THE CRUEL KISS

TATENDA CHARLES MUNYUKI

By The Same Author

XCLUSIVE ZONE ANGELS: The Chosen Ones
XCLUSIVE ZONE ANGELS: The Adamant Genesis
XCLUSIVE ZONE ANGELS: The Odd Temptations
XCLUSIVE ZONE ANGELS: The Sacred Secrets
LOTANDO UREY: The Torture Chamber
LOTANDO UREY: Servitude Defined
GREEN ROSES: Petals and Thorns
The Naked Teenager
The Angry Girlchild
The Cruel Kiss
Inhumanity

NACH (The Adventures of Nathan Amanda Chenai Hama) BOOK SERIES
THE MONTE CHICKS BOOK SERIES
BATTLE OF SEXES BOOK SERIES
PU$HERZ BOOK SERIES

THE CRUEL KISS

TATENDA CHARLES MUNYUKI

Harp Bookz International

The Cruel Kiss

First published in Zimbabwe in 2014
Harp Bookz International
an imprint of Tatenda Charles Munyuki Publishing

ISBN   978 0 7974 6165 9

Printed and bound by Harp Bookz International, Harare,
Zimbabwe.
harpbookz@gmail.com

facebook.com/tatendacmunyuki

www.tcmpublishingzim.com

To all conspiracy buffs…

Chapter One

What do we know about ourselves, our history – our memories? I think we know practically nothing.

On the day I was born, the doctors claimed that I was going to be blind. It wasn't something my father absorbed in too well for two days later, he was said to have committed suicide by blowing his brains out using a grenade. Wherever he got that small weapon of destruction, only my crime-related *uncle* knew.

Given the circumstance that I was a successfully born unwanted ankle-biter, my mother threw up when the lady doctor told her what she had produced. It was worse enough that she had had me, being blind too only opened my already negative entrance to a world of unrest.

At least that was what I thought – or the truth I knew – for a long-time. Little did I really know that it does take a considerable amount of time to know that a baby is really blind. So where did I get these silly stories from? Well, they did make sense when I thought of them – more than anything else did for me to justify where my biological parents were.

Three months after being born, I was dumped in a deserted park close to the shops of a suburb called Chisipite, wrapped in a cotton blanket with a tight t-shirt and fluffy small pants, nothing covering both my head and toes.

Ms Parkinson just happened to be taking her evening walk when she came across me whimpering from hunger and the desire of warmth. Two months later, when nobody claimed me to be theirs, I was christened *Jewel Dean Parkinson*.

Ms Parkinson was what you called a modern day loner. She was sixty-four years old by the time I was born and dumped. Her main home was fixed in hills of Chisipite, constructed to exist for centuries. She had inherited the big house from her mother from a great-line of ancestors since the colonial era. Ms Harriet

Parkinson had never married, but had been blessed with a son who had unfortunately been stolen from her one sad rainy night. He had overdosed.

The old lady brought me up like her own for twenty years until she passed away. It had taken me two years to recover from my grief. She had meant the whole world to me and she still did. I had inherited the Parkinsons' mansion including a healthy sum of money Ms Parkinson had saved for my old age.

I had grown up being the misfit. I was either the blind boy in the neighbourhood, the blind boy to many of the girls I *saw*, the blind boy to those who knew me one way or the other and I lived a life of being underrated in many dimensions of life.

I was blind, yes, that was true in a sense, but I had an awesome secret that only Ms Parkinson had known and had taken to her grave. I could *see* as very much as a person with normal eyes, but saw in a unique way.

Chapter Two

The eyes I possessed weren't normal.

It was a medical phenomenon – if it was ever publicised. It began when I was seven years old. I had woken up one late night to have a glass of water. My room was situated next to Ms Parkinson's for the main reason of her being able to hear me if I somehow cried for her help during the night. Less did she know that, on few nights, I experienced mysterious heatwaves that woke me. On those nights, I used my walking stick to find my way to the kitchen and, using my sensory skills, poured myself some water from our huge fridge, which was custom designed for me.

In simpler terms, what started to happen was that I could *see* with my eyes closed. It sounded a little bit silly at first when I finally presented the matter to Ms Parkinson, for I couldn't see with my eyes open. It seemed like my eyelids acted as some kind of special vision giving instruments. Although the vision was a bit blurry at first, by nine years old I could clearly see anything as long as I had my eyelids closed. In fear of not wanting to seem like a freak, I kept this secret to myself. Ms Parkinson did the same. She was mainly scared that if we visited any medical institution in search of answers, I would probably have been made a human lab rat.

I wore dark glasses and still used my stick despite having that ability to see where I was going. At first, it was immensely difficult to keep my eyelids shut and not automatically open them, but in the end my senses self-trained themselves to keep my eyelids shut during the day and open during the night as I slept. Ms Parkinson always joked that I looked like an owl as I slept and it always comforted me that she could find some humour on such a bizarre situation. By the age of seventeen, she had even taught me how to drive her car around the house and in the neighbourhood. She had bought a new car with dark tinted windows mainly for this purpose.

Designated as blind gave me the privileges of learning quite a lot of stuff. I had learnt to use all my senses to great heights as a blind person is required to and naturally does as the years pass. I could smell a rat from meters away, feel and differentiate textures of all sorts, taste liquids and be able to tell what was what and had an amazing hearing ability.

The ladies never guessed that I could very much see them when I looked at them. Of course to all I was blind. They did all kinds of stuff in front of me. At one time, a university associate of mine invited me to her house for what she called a studying sleepover. She had the nerve of changing all her clothes in front of me. It took me a month to erase her nakedness from my mind, but that act had started another chapter of my life. It searched for the man in me and many who have passed through them really know that late adolescent years are a bitch.

After my white mother's death, I was left with an awesome amount of wealth that opened many doors of temptation. I spent two whole years enjoying my inheritance, partly in solitude. Fat grew on me as I barely left the house and ate a lot. That fat took me another two years to get rid of. It wasn't easy finding a job being blind so I didn't try to find one. The disabled society was often neglected amongst the employed majority. I did create my own kind of job. I specialised on hiring people. I employed them. That was after I spent four years studying Financial Management through open distance learning. I was twenty-five when I got my MBA and was a *bachelor* for sure.

I was too single the few friends that I had were calling me gay. My lady of the house – the one who made sure my house was kept in a mint condition – did her best to try to hook me up. Mrs Maguma had given up when she realised that I wasn't the least interested in women. *What kind of woman would love a blind man?* If there was, I didn't want to create an offspring of genetically modified kids who could see with their eyelids closed.

However, there was this lady that I tried hard not to like. She lived in my neighbourhood – the daughter of a very wealthy businessperson. She was called Ruth Tariro and she was beautiful on both sides. We had particularly grown up together, attended the same schools and church.

Talking about church, I had stopped going years back in cowardice of seeing her and being tempted – apart from my mother no longer forcing me to attend after her death. Ruth wasn't a church girl. Well, I mean your ordinary kind of a church girl. She believed in God, but she argued with the ethics of all churches and religion. She was in other words a heavily pronounced sceptic. Many claimed her to be contentious, but then she was a hotshot young and successful journalist. She spoke her mind no matter whom it touched.

Ruth was like my frequent visitor. She said she loved my house, my company and I only wondered why. Mrs Maguma had a habit of calling her over for little things. She and Ruth's mother were great friends. When Ruth visited, I found myself locked up in my study pretending to be busy whilst listening hard for her departure. Mrs Maguma always used her spare key to unlock the door and lock the two of us in.

Perhaps Ruth liked my presumed handsomeness with my dark glasses on or she was just attracted by my status. As I owned a self-made bank, money really was my language. They called me *the Blind Banker.*

I was rich, black and had an English name.

That was who I was only yesterday before I woke up on the sofa of my huge office with blood all over me. Ruth's mother and father lay intimately on my desk and they weren't having sex. They were corpses.

CHAPTER THREE

It was timeless for I couldn't even remember the last time I ate or even stopped shivering. With the long-hooded jacket covering my blood-stained shirt, I was currently lingering on a corner somewhere around where the CBD ended and the wide long roads began. At that time of the day, Harare buzzes with people. It was night-time and, with many going home from businesses and a few coming to enjoy the night at restaurants and whatever possible, I found it pretty awkward that nobody had seen me and not known. Somehow, I felt déjà vu, as if I had to be there for a reason – as if it was the place to be. I produced my wallet and looked inside. There were three hundred dollar notes and two fifties. *Not enough money to disappear*, I thought.

I tried hard not to think at the moment. Big trouble was what I was in, but I tried hard not to think at all. With four hundred dollars in my pocket, I could only assume that I would not last for a month, even if I weren't officially on the run by then. My mind scattered and finally rested on the notion of a good hideout. The only place I could think of acquiring accommodation without much fuss was a low-key hotel and possibly a motel. Any hotel that I could access nearby, be it flamboyant or not, would sniff and swallow up my cash in the blink of an eye.

Twenty or so minutes passed as I looked around, my mind in fast forward trying to formulate the best way forward. Part of me suddenly quacked and vibrated, ultimately waking me up from my apparent unending thoughts. It took me a while to realise that it was my nine hundred dollar iPhone, a realisation that I was currently a thousand bucks wealthy.

The caller's ID nearly gave me a heart attack. My vision automatically went to the phone's timer. It was eight-twenty evening time. There was no possible way the bodies couldn't have been found by now.

I had left my office in a demented hurry and if I had at least thought things through, I would have at best locked my door. Quite a few people had seen me leave in my hooded jacket, mainly reserved for winter, and I knew that I had appeared a bit odd then. That kind of thinking made me shiver. *What I had woken up to, was it for real?* The cellphone kept on vibrating in my hand with Ruth's number flashing on it.

Perhaps I had panicked after a terrible brief hallucination and reacted badly, I thought with some hope. *Why would Ruth be calling me if half-naked bodies of her parents had been found dead in my office?* Nothing made sense to me at all. The phone suddenly gave up after a few minutes of my negligence to answer it. I dialled my home number and it took two anxious minutes before someone answered. It was Mrs Maguma.

'Good evening, Mrs Maguma,' I said in the most controlled voice I could manage.

What sounded like a chocked scream came from the other end.

'Dean, Dean,' Mrs Maguma cried. 'Dean, are you alright? Oh, Dean, I have been worried sick about you. Where are you?'

That unsettling reaction, together with the string of words given made me more anxious. 'I'm okay, Mrs Maguma, I have –'

'Dean, what in the world is going on?' Mrs Maguma cut me short. 'The police have been looking for you. They aren't telling me anything, but by the way they are operating, they really want to see you at all costs. Did anything bad happen at the bank?'

All the hope I had managed to gather was erased at that moment. I felt like I was going to faint as my brain failed to process the confusion that now colonised it. The cellphone felt like dumbbell in my hand as I fought hard to keep it close to my ear.

A pretty lady carrying a laptop bag over one shoulder, dressed neatly in a black suit suddenly emerged in the path I was lingering. In an effort to keep my head down and look unsuspicious, I ended up leaning close to the walls of an adjacent building. The lady saw this kind of weird reaction and slowed down, nearly stopping. With my hood on, I looked like someone ready to mug her. It was the kind of attention I didn't need now.

With Mrs Maguma saying something from the phone, I slowly tossed my hood over, exposing my dark glasses. The action seemed to settle the lady, but seconds later, she picked up her pace as she figured me harmless. Caught in a moment of madness, I tried to encourage her trust with a smile. That only provoked her attention further as she stared more closely at me.

'Mrs Maguma, please calm down,' I said, reconnecting my focus to her.

Mrs Maguma wasn't calming down in any form of way. She gave my ear a great deal of noise-abuse as she went on and on about the police and many other things I couldn't hear.

'Excuse me, are you okay?'

I looked up and was stunned back against the wall as the lady stood close to me as if she had been zoomed in. My glasses nearly fell and I struggled to put them back on without dropping my phone.

'Mrs Maguma, can you hold on for a moment, please,' I said and placed my free palm on the phone's microphone. 'Excuse me, what did you say?' I said to the lady. As my closed eyes made her outline a bit better from the dark, as she was now closer, I wondered if I was having another hallucination. Correction, my first one, as that scene was probably going to make me the unluckiest of bastards. 'Mrs Maguma, I'll call you back.'

The definition of a beautiful young woman was totally nuked because what I saw, I can't define in words. There are probably a dozen words to define and describe a woman's beauty and none of them fitted what I saw.

'Your shirt, are you hurt?' the lady said pointing towards the base of my jacket.

Looking down, I saw my shirt lingering at my waist from my new jacket. The sudden sight of blood on it made my heart stop. 'My elbow got injured at work today,' I said hastily tucking in my shirt.

'Oh, sorry,' the lady looked up at me. Her eyes in the dark had some sort of gleam. She looked like she wanted to ask me more, but couldn't and, from the way her eyes scanned me, I could tell that she was shy.

'Are you single?' The question came from my mouth like an exhale. It even shook me. *What the hell?* I thought taken back by my nerve.

The lady was stunned and that maybe an understatement. Her nose wrinkled and the gleam in her eyes turned to flames. 'What?'

'I'm in a bit of tight spot, lady, and I'm looking for a place to crash for the night,' I said, not wasting anytime.

For me, it was a do or die at the moment. I needed help and if this lady could assist me by giving me a bed for a night, it was okay.

The lady stared at me, her face transforming into many expressions. It gave me enough time to study her. She was probably in her mid-twenties and by the way she dressed, possibly one of those fresh graduates working for an NGO. That idea was supported by the laptop she was carrying. If she was single or not, I couldn't exactly point it out, but she wore no ring. My hopes were laid on her being one of those modern independent women.

If my estimates were correct, that meant hope and I truly needed lots of it, not mentioning too much luck wouldn't be a bad phase in my life at that moment.

'I know that we have just met, but I really need help,' I begged in a firm tone.

'You don't expect me to help a stranger in that way, do you?' the lady said shrugging. She showed signs of hesitancy.

If what I did was stupid, then it was an omen of black. What later scared me was that I didn't even consider the consequences. 'My name is Jewel Dean Parkinson,' I told her.

'The Blind Banker?'

Those three words froze me at different dimensions. My eyes were set on her as if I could see normally. I didn't look blind at all. I thought I saw a glimpse of a grin on her face. After all that had happened between us in the few minutes, I couldn't be labelled as blind man to an observing mind.

'That's what some people call me.'

The lady showed that she didn't believe me. 'But, you aren't blind,' she gaped.

Very smart, I discovered. I wanted help so lying wasn't an option. *But how could I explain that I could see with my eyes closed and not seem like I was joking or mocking her?* 'It's a long story ma'am, but seriously I need help. Will you help me?' I said, my voice stressed a bit of desperation in it.

We exchanged stares for a long time. The few people who passed by where we were just looked on wondering if we were night stalkers or a couple that had just had an argument. I was scared of a lot of things. If this lady refused to help me, and when the police started to look for me on a wider scale by using the media, would she present herself to the authorities and inform them that she had seen me? Moreover, by that time, what would have happened to me? I prayed to whichever god there was to claim me from the abyss of misfortune.

CHAPTER FOUR

The local officials didn't mess around and they nailed me. My face was infamous all over from six in the morning. It was publicised that I was wanted for questioning towards the brutal homicide involving the murder of well-known business magnate Obey Tariro and his wife. The police wanted to know if I was still alive for they had found drops of blood matching my DNA on the crime scene. They however didn't mention where the crime scene was or the exact way they had found Ruth's parents. I was officially a wanted person and Division – Criminal Investigation Division – was claimed to be the ones leading on the case. That was nothing, but bad news for me. Agents from Division were serious business.

Barbara-Jean Maya was indeed single and independent. Her apartment identified her as someone who lived a stable life, untainted by male prospects. She even had a pet cat called Fluffy. Fluffy was very aggressive at first, raising her white fur and long tail when she saw me. That night I slept in fear that she was going to suddenly attack me whilst I had my nightmares.

Fears of being attacked by a cat could have appeared unrealistic considering the crap that moulded my ass, but BJ's habitat had such a warm relaxing feel to it that I actually felt at home the moment I stepped into it – despite Fluffy's hisses.

Why this sweet lady had agreed to help me was beyond my understanding, but I was so grateful. She had given me her sofa to sleep on after providing me with one of the best meals I ever had. Maybe it was because of the hunger that ate me up that evening. To me – no offence – but Mrs Maguma was the best cook around. She had a way of making unforgettable meals on a daily basis.

If sleep were defined by closing your eyes whilst lying on some surface or in my case, opening your eyes, I would say I slept like a baby. Then if we present other contexts like dreaming and being barely conscious, well I didn't sleep a wink. I spent the whole night hosting a quiz with my mind. A quiz that lacked answers. The biggest question of them all was probably the first one I had ever asked myself. *Why had I woken up in my office with blood all over my shirt with Ruth's parents indecently dead on my desk?* I thought of many explanations, but none was the least satisfying.

That morning, BJ stood in front of me wearing a t-shirt that was labelled *UNICEF* on the middle in blue from its whiteness and below she wore a short that gave me a nice view of her gorgeously shaped long legs – possibly her nightclothes. Her appearance had me cough a bit.

'This is what you call *a bit of a tight spot?*' she said, rather shouted at me pointing at my photo, which was being shown on the morning news. She looked pale.

'I – er,' was the response I gave, not knowing how to explain the shit I was sunk in.

'You are wanted for murder, goddamn it!'

I just sat there ashamed. I wondered how many more sentences would come next before she asked me to leave before or after she called the police.

'What kind of person are you?' BJ cried out, backing away from me as if distancing herself for safety's sake. 'First of all, you fool people that you are blind –'

'I can see with my eyes closed,' I said simply.

'Then you – what did you say?' she stuttered back, playing back my words in her head. 'Is this some kind of game to you? Now I'm beginning to believe you are a sociopath.'

'Why haven't you called the police on me?' I asked when curiosity got the better of me.

She knew that I could see, although not how. *Wouldn't she be afraid, especially after knowing what I was now infamous for?* That like shut her up for a few seconds. She screwed her face into a frown that made her look different. For a moment, after a new glimpse of her lovely face, I thought she was fighting a grin.

'People who kill people don't tell others to please calm down and not appear violent at the same time.'

'What?' I said confused.

'Yesterday, on your phone, you told Mrs Mag-something to calm down. You sounded as if you were talking to your mother and yet she wasn't,' BJ said taking a long towel and shyly covered her legs. 'I'm no profiler, but there is something about you that excludes you from the world of murderers.'

I was dumbfounded. Of all people, a stranger trusted me enough to ignore the most devastating picture one can ever be presented with. It seemed too unreal. My attention rested on the TV and saw my bank being shown by the broadcast as they told the world at large who I was. I rose up and firmly positioned my glasses on. I produced my wallet and slipped out a hundred-dollar bill.

'Barbara Jean, have I got that correct?' I said.

'Barbara-Jean, like one word,' she grinned.

'Jean, Dean – isn't that a bit queer?' I said, subconsciously noting the oddity or coincidence. 'Sounds like we are from a nursery rhyme book.'

BJ giggled. 'That is exactly what you said when dated,' she said and then looked away quickly.

'Dated?' I looked at her confused. *What was she talking about?*

'Forget I said that – what are you holding out that money for?' she said staring at the note.

'Here, Barbara – thanks for everything,' I said offering the note.

BJ looked at me surprised. 'What's that for? I don't want your money, Dean.'

It was the first time she ever said my name. Boy did it rock my senses. 'Please take it,' I persuaded her, knowing that when the time came, I was going to regret this generosity.

Three hundred dollars wasn't going to be enough to get me out of the country safely. At least without being caught that was. It seemed the only possible option in my quandary.

'Dean, I said I don't want your money,' BJ shouted, her temper escalating again. 'And what are you doing?'

'Leaving,' I said calmly, gratefully reuniting the hundred-dollar bill with the other two. 'I can't risk putting you in any kind of danger. If the police know that I am here, you'll be arrested and charged for aiding a criminal.'

BJ laughed sarcastically. It made her eyes glitter. I felt momentarily weak. A loud knock on the door brought me back to my senses. I jerked as BJ's head twisted towards the door. The knock came again, louder this time and we looked at each other.

BJ pointed towards a small corridor that led to the rest of the apartment and mouthed the words "my bedroom, now." Not knowing which it was, I dashed in that direction and made two misses until I finally found it at the end of the corridor on the left.

The room was so feminine, I nearly giggled. She even had two teddy bears on her bed and lying peacefully between them was Fluffy. She sensed me enter and raised her head. We stared at each other like vowed enemies and when she growled, my heart seemed to halt, then beat faster. I glued myself to the door and what I heard made me forget about Fluffy for some time.

BJ's visitor was a workmate who had dropped in as a surprise to take her to work. It was a man and a very cocky one from what I heard. Chris was his name and he appeared to be BJ's pursuer. It could have been all good, but the fact that he was suffering from a one-sided crush made it worse. BJ's responses to his charm were so cold that I too even felt iced-up. Chris went on the I don't know-eth time trying to charm his way to a good day, but BJ cut him like stone. I heard quite a lot of stuff I wished I hadn't. This dude seemed to have been campaigning for thy lady's heart for a year now with no success. I noticed why he was failing horribly. He was a jerk. Every word that came from his mouth was full of flattery and pride, aimed to impress BJ. Most of what he said compelled me to giggle.

Fluffy scratched my jean so hard that her paws found their way to my ankle's skin. By impulse, I pulled my leg hard in pain and the ultimate action was my shoe kicking the door. The sound made me panic, and Fluffy too took it as a sign for aggressiveness towards her. She growled fiercely. The fracas we made got the attention of the others who stopped arguing. Fluffy tried at best to attack me, something I think she had been itching to do since we met and I did manage to avoid her sharp claws. When she sprung at me for the fourth time, I luckily caught hold of her and instantaneously threw her out of an open window with a perfectness that amazed me.

'So you got someone over?' I heard Chris shout. He wasn't pleased.

'I don't have anyone over,' BJ said in a voice that wondered what was going on in her bedroom.

'Don't lie to me, Jean,' Chris said.

He sounded like a jealous boyfriend. I hoped that he wouldn't demand to see whom it was for I was confident that he would try at all cost to be some kind of hero by handing me over to the police if he knew they were looking for me yet.

'If I had someone over, seriously he'd have asked what the hell you were doing in my apartment,' BJ said smartly. 'Now if you don't want me reporting for inappropriate misconduct to your supervisor, leave.'

Chris left after grumbling a lot and I felt my heart surface. I went over to the bedroom's window and saw him leave in an expensive Mercedes. From what I could see, peeping cautiously from floors up, he was a jerk, but a very handsome one. It was hard to contemplate why BJ hadn't fallen for his chiselled looks.

'Oh, God, I'm late,' I heard BJ say, rushing towards the bedroom.

I stepped back from the window and tried to compose my guilty expression into an innocent one.

Barbara-Jean looked flushed as she opened the door. Her unnerved expression attracted me more that I ended staring at the mirror. What I saw made me look down. I looked silly in a pink t-shirt BJ had given me the previous night after I had secretly washed and hid the one that had been marred with whoever's blood.

'Your boyfriend?' I asked teasingly.

'In my worst nightmares,' BJ gasped looking around in search of something. A stranded meow fused through the open window. 'Oh, Dean, what did you do?' she cried pushing me aside rushing for the window. 'Fluffy, Fluffy!' she called out to her cat.

'I, er – am sorry –'

'Get out, Dean, get out!' she shouted at me.

I didn't need second telling. I was out of the room in a flash. The shoes were on my feet the moment I sat on the sofa to wear them. I wore my long hooded jacket swiftly and rose to leave. It was sad to leave this way, but I knew I had to.

Maybe one day we would meet again under normal circumstances, I thought sadly.

I was about to open the main door to go when I heard BJ coming from her room. My curiosity forced me to have one last look at her.

'Where are you going?' she erupted. She was now in a fresh black suit, her laptop bag ready on her shoulder.

I stopped short, confused. 'I'm leaving, I –'

'No you are not,' she said and pushed the door shut.

She stood in front of me and my highly sensitive nose picked up her enticing perfume, which must have been poured on her to hide the fact that she hadn't bathed. I looked down frowning at her. She frowned back.

'You won't last a week before they catch you. I don't know what actually happened, but I know for sure how the justice system works. When something like this happens, someone has to be the doer and for now, it is you.'

Her wisdom amazed me. 'That's exactly what I was thinking, Barbara. And, would you want to be beside someone you have known for less than twenty-four hours and yet trust enough to try to protect them? I can't have you fall because of me. This is Division we are talking about.'

'Please make yourself at home,' BJ said ignoring everything I had just said as if I hadn't said it at all. 'We'll discuss this when I return from work.'

With that, she was out before I could react. The keys on the door swayed back and forth, creating the only noise in the space. Five minutes passed before I fully recovered. *Was this some kind of joke?* The woman had left me in her apartment, me a wanted person for that matter. I got suspicious as the seconds passed. *What was going to stop her from calling the police and tell them where I was?* I opened the door about to leave. I couldn't move, my mind pulling me in two different directions. I closed the door and locked it, strolled to the sofa I had slept on and let myself fall on it heaving a sigh. I was a lost puppy with a wag-less tail.

CHAPTER FIVE

Five o'clock evening time arrived and I had spent the whole day devising a plan. I had made it a point not to switch the TV on for the daily news broadcasts weren't something I desired. My stomach grumbled with hunger and then did I realize that I hadn't ate anything that day. Stomach necessities had seemed to be the last thing on my mind.

I did however hear a soft meow around ten in the morning coming from the door associated with scratches. I had thought hard and found a carton of some fresh milk in the fridge and a tin can of cat food. Using one of BJ's bowls, I had poured some of the milk and smelly cat food in it and opened the door. Things between Fluffy and me had changed from then on. We were now the best of buddies. At the time being, she was cuddling on the sofa, a distance from me sleeping or doing whatever cats do to relax.

Papers scribbled in my rushed banker's longhand filled the top of the sitting room's glass table as if a writer was rewriting a bad script. It was all messy and I hoped my host wouldn't freak out at the sight.

My plan was pretty vague for it was too tight in its setup. My first idea was to find out what had really happened. My last ideas were to clear my name. The other ideas in-between were barely idealistic. I figured that when I put things into motion, everything would start to enthuse smoothly or roughly whatever the case. I barely had friends in high places. The only high-up friend I ever had was Ruth's father who had been a very influential businessman. Now the police and Division wanted me because he was found dead in my office. *How ironic could life ever get?*

To discover what had happened, I needed the skills of a sleuth and I was no detective. The skills I had were money skills and, perhaps to an extent, people skills. I had a way with people, especially those who took me for a real person not a blind banker.

I wish I knew a detective or anyone who had connections with the Law. I had written down possible causes of what I now called "the deadly sin". One of the possibilities was a blackout. *Had I blacked out, sleepwalked and killed the Tariros? If so, how could I have done it? But then, seriously, why would I have done it?* I was scared of Ruth because of the unstable attraction that had existed between us. I knew Ruth liked or even loved me then, before I supposedly murdered her parents. In spite of all that, I had had a very strong relationship with her parents. They had adored me, respected me and even cherished me like a son of theirs. I was the blind boy who had made it big and my so-called humbleness had given me more points on their judge. In return, I truly had liked the Tariros. They were the few amongst the not much people who had treated me the way I wanted – like a human being. *Why would I kill them and make them pose in a most horrific way, in my office of all places?*

The second part of the plan claimed or assessed a third party. Someone had set me up. *For what reason?* To me, that seemed like the most attractive idea for it exonerated me. But then, it wasn't as easy as that. More questions came and they led to many more. I had no enemies, or at least thought I had none. *Who would benefit from my devastation and why Ruth's parents, why kill them – in an extremely disturbing manner?*

I was suddenly caught napping when the door suddenly opened. My heart raced then relaxed a little at the sight of Barbara-Jean. Her smile made my heart swell with emotion, a kind of feeling I experienced for the first time. She was carrying grocery bags and I dashed over to assist her. Fluffy sensed her madam's sudden return and raised her funny head. Jubilantly, the cat leapt from the sofa and ran to BJ.

Barbara thrust the grocery bags into my arms and picked her pet, fussing it in the funniest way. I grinned at the sight and went to release the load.

'Hi, BJ – how was your day?' I greeted her as she walked in behind me.

She looked up at me and knelt down to let Fluffy on the ground. 'Oh, hi, Dean. I had a busy day. What about you? How did you spend your first day as a fugitive in my tiny apartment?' she said rolling her eyes.

I laughed and felt good for somehow all the stress within me mitigated. 'An honest day without curtains,' I said in a drooling tone.

My body was tight in her pink t-shirt and my baggy jeans. The jacket was the only fresh thing on me for it wasn't more than a day old. BJ gazed around the kitchen and her eyes later lingered on the container of milk I had forgotten to refrigerate. She looked at me then at Fluffy and grinned.

'I see that you two must have come to an understanding. That's good,' Barbara said opening her fridge. 'It looks like you haven't eaten anything. Are you planning on starving yourself?'

'If it gets me out of this shithole I am in, I can do nothing worse,' I replied with such tenacity, an unplanned outburst I later felt ashamed of.

Barbara's humour didn't faze off though. 'It's good to know that you are actually doing something about it,' she said, heading for her bedroom.

As Barbara prepared dinner, I exchanged life stories with her. She was very geared up to provide me with hers. Barbara-Jean Maya came from a family of three. Her mother who was now a widow, her brother who was four years older than her and she the only daughter. Her dad had passed away when she was twelve and from the way she spoke about her family, it was a loving family and a wealthy one for that matter. Michael Maya was an intelligence practitioner who developed computer software for a major medical firm and various other firms. BJ's brother was married with a baby coming along the way. Mike was more of BJ's idol. I wondered how Mike would react if he knew that his sister was keeping home a wanted person.

When I started to tell her my story, BJ and I were sitting at the sofa eating. I espied her expressions change as I related to her how I grew up to be a misfit. I left out most of the details that would have appeared weird to her.

'But I don't understand, Dean,' she said placing her plate on the glass table, a distance away from my papers which I had neatly arranged at one corner. She used a dishtowel to wipe her hands and folded her left leg sitting on it on the sofa whilst resting her back at her end of the sofa to gaze at me. 'You can see and yet what you have told me makes you a blind person.'

I swallowed hard and slowly looked at her. She had changed into a white t-shirt and grey sweatpants. My heart pumped like a locomotive train. Her long brunette hair falling over her face made her seem like… I practically had no word to describe it for *"an Angel"* would be an insincere description. With her eyes looking directly at me, I felt naked and vulnerable.

Would she understand the truth? I quizzed over it. The woman deserved nothing, but the truth from me. Every police officer and Division Agent in the country was looking for me and this woman was making me dinner.

'I'm not lying to you, BJ,' I said. 'You have to believe what I'm about to tell you no matter how insane it may sound.'

Barbara's eyes peered on me hard. She nodded her head, prompting me to say whatever I was going to say. I braced myself and placed my plate beside hers on the glass table. She handed me the dishtowel with a weak smile. I took it and let my eyesight focus on the dark screen of the unpowered television which showed our reflections. I told her my secret.

'You must be teasing me, right?' BJ said after my confessions. The look on her face told me that she didn't believe me.

I took off my glasses for the first time in her presence and stared at her with my eyelids closed. 'As you can see, my eyes are closed. Do anything and I'll tell you exactly what you did?'

After a moment of hesitation, Barbara raised her middle finger at me frowning. I smiled at her.

'I thought you were an immaculate lady, why give me the f-word with your finger?'

BJ looked stunned for a while, and then returned the smile.

'You are smiling,' I told her, 'and now you are bewildered, brushing your hair from your face with your left hand which basically means you use your left hand for writing. You are now pinching your nose, lolling your tongue out for me, closing your ears with both your hands, pointing towards the TV, the corridor to your bedroom and well, folding your hands with a frustrated expression.'

BJ settled into a comfortable position by tucking in her leg further into the sofa. 'How do you do that? Is that some sort of a trick?' she said, doubt still present in her voice.

'No, Barbie, I can see with my eyelids closed,' I said and opened my eyes. I saw nothing.

'So you mean to tell me you can't see me now?'

I shrugged. 'Yes, I don't see a thing.'

I heard a few swooshing sounds and after three or so minutes, I heard the first signs of acceptance.

'Good Lord, your eyes look normal, but you truly can't see. There is no way you could have let me take my shirt off in front of you and not blink an inch. Even the fork a few inches from your eye stimulated nothing.'

'What?' I closed my eyelids and looked at her. She was in the process of adjusting her t-shirt. Some part of me felt like I had missed quite a lot by opening my eyes. 'You put a fork to what – er, do you want to make me blind?'

Barbara giggled and shook her head. 'How can I make you blind, Mr Blind Banker, when you are already blind?' she said tauntingly. 'But, wow, this is something like a sci-fi show. You can see with your eyes closed. The world is truly full of amazing things,' she said her hand on her chin, her gaze far away in a thoughtful distance.

'If they surpass you, Barbie-J, I'd be damned. What's more amazing than… you? If there is, I'd truly be amazed,' I said unrehearsed.

The words just flew out from my mouth that they left me confused the moment I produced them. *Now why would I commit myself like that?* I thought cursing myself.

Wearing her thoughtful expression, I was a little relieved thinking that she hadn't heard me. As the expression turned into a grin then from a grin into a smile, her face beaming, I cursed myself more.

'Barbie-J, hey?' she said, rising from her thoughts.

'I meant Barbara,' I choked, not looking at her.

'I like it,' Barbara said her eyes fixed on me. I felt the emotion in them and trembled.

'What is it?' I asked my voice shaky. I swallowed again and my throat responded.

'The *Barbie-J*, I like it,' she said and rose up.

I too rose automatically. The air between us had fierce strong waves that brought the two of us together like magnets from unlike poles. My eyes closed, I smelt baby powder on her. It made my nose grow bigger as the scent poured in uncontrollably. The look in her eyes was suggestive. She wanted me to make the first move. As much as I ached for it that everything on me hurt as if I was on fire, I couldn't move.

It wasn't my previous encounters or my presents that prevented me from acting. It was what stood in front of me. We were both willing to go that extra mile, our bodies were vibrating for it, but something told me that it wouldn't be right. It would be my first time having sex for real, losing my virginity perhaps to cause this lady pregnant with a genetically dissimulated offspring, was more like a dog thing, and I was by no means a dog. Ms Parkinson had taught me a lot and I didn't have any reserve of wicked thoughts to insult her memory.

Fornicating on magazines, lust web pages or whatever that adolescent-minded was one thing. Doing it for real was another. Somewhere deep down in my heart I felt like what my life was now or was going to become in the following days was all for a reason and letting my emotional desires take control over me that moment wasn't the reason.

I stepped over and hugged Barbara. For someone who had been expecting more, Barbara was weak in my arms. I mastered some strength and whispered a "thank you," in her ear. I walked over to the door, opened it and closed it swiftly behind me. Using the keys, I had in my pocket, I locked the door, wore my glasses, my hood, and ran downstairs. I made sure that I left the keys safely fitted in the lock as I glanced back at BJ's apartment door and left. I had a mess to get out off and perhaps after that, I would revisit these last two days of my life on which the heavens had ironically tested me by presenting *the lady*.

Chapter Six

It's really hard to ignore how religion messes up with your head when you are in a dilemma. The most excruciating of times are possibly the most revealing of times of whether one does or doesn't believe in God, in Jesus and in life itself.

I sat in the small room belonging to an old motel sited in a suburb called Hatfield. My fears of being made out by the many people who had watched my photo being mercilessly broadcast on the news had been iced for no one from the path linking BJ's flat and my brief traverse to Hatfield had looked at me twice. My mind brazed on the idea that my travelling at night had lessened the odds of detection.

Sitting on the only possible sitting place in the room, I had my head in my hands thinking of how my life had gone from gleam to gloom like a beautiful sunny day clouded by a thunderstorm. I did believe in God, just as I believed that for a population to grow, pregnant women were needed. What was hard for me to attain was faith. My faith was shambles of doubt. In a world of more than a billion people, some born and some dying each second, how did God know all of us and even could count every hair on every head?

Was this my test of faith? I thought. Assuming it was, I was confident that I was going to fail. I was a living testimony of supernatural works. I was also a living testimony that faith doesn't sprout overnight. It takes seconds from the ultimate breath of one's life to have 100% faith and, as much as I wished death upon myself, I could never seem more alive than birth.

My principals were currently varied. I was specifically without purpose, commonly without a vision. My problems were classified allergies that discovered the weakness in me and ate their way through my mental capability.

The dimness of the room seeped into my consciousness. I had found it wise to let the light rest for the day and save the motel's electricity by habiting in the dark. My attention was distracted by the whiteness of the pile of papers I had stationed beside me. I had left Barbara's place abruptly without carrying along the papers that had contained my overall sketchy plan. This meant planning all over again. I couldn't stay focused enough to take the room's pen and draft another plan as similar as the one I had done before. Loss of hope defeated my senses. *Was this irrational fear?*

I picked up my phone and called home. Mrs Maguma answered the phone and when she heard my voice, she let the phone receiver clutter to the phone's small table. A few seconds passed before I heard her voice, a voice that was moulded with repressed fear.

'Dean, Dean, is that you? Jewel Dean Parkinson, is that you?' she was hypnotized now.

I understood what she felt and my heart shrunk to pea size. 'I didn't do it, Mrs Maguma. *Why would I do it, how could I do it?* I am innocent, Mrs Maguma. Please tell me that you believe me,' I said as calmly as I could. I needed her faith.

It was possibly going to be one of my strongest motivations if I was going to make it through the wildfire. Seconds of no response made me weak, drugged by anxiety at its remarkable worst.

'I believe you, Dean. I swear with my life that you didn't do it,' Mrs Maguma finally said.

I felt like someone being told that they had just won a million dollars with no tax in it. Shock and joy all in the same package, confusion icing it up. Tears flooded my closed eyes and I had to open them to let them fall.

'Thank you, tha… nk you,' I stuttered.

I told her what had happened to me, but left BJ's part. There was no telling if the cops had somehow succeeded in getting a warrant to plant surveillance devices at my home. It was prudent to play it safe. I would have never forgiven myself if I let Miss Maya get into trouble.

Mrs Maguma begged me to turn myself over to the police before I got hurt or something severe. It would have taken me decades to convince Mrs Maguma that I could take care of myself. To her, I was a blind thirty-four-year-old trying to flee from the authorities. She interrogated me on how I had managed to stay at large for so long without being caught. As someone who didn't know my secret, I let her believe it was God's hand guiding me. A committed Christian she was, she believed me.

I made the call around midnight and it wasn't an emotional experience, but a commanded action. It was inevitable that I had to make it no matter what it led to. Before I made the call, I wondered if the police had put someone at my mobile network service provider's offices to monitor my phone calls and possibly triangulate my whereabouts. As once a successful banker, I had two lines and my phone had a double SIM facility that catered for both. One line was in my name, the other I had brought it from a street vender. The latter I used for my private and vital communications. I used that one to call Ruth.

'Ruth,' was the first word I said to her.

Ruth must have been asleep, exhausted from grief because it took her a while to distinguish my voice. The balm in her voice shaved me bald.

'Why didn't you answer your phone when I called you, Jew?' She said. I was always Jewel or more precisely Jew to her.

My tongue was solid. I couldn't move it to say all the things that saturated my mind. I was the man who was wanted for her parents' murders. *What could I say?*

'I know you didn't do it, Jew, you…' Ruth said and the last word was echoed with the emotion I had been expecting from the beginning, '…loved them just as they loved you. You were like a son to them.' Despair chocked her words.

So far, everybody I had talked to believed I was innocent. Maybe it wasn't so bad to turn myself over to the police, I assessed. 'Thank you,' I said. 'It means so much to me to know that you trust me that much. I'm sorry about them, Ruth. I'm truly sorry.' The words came from my throat as tears flowed down my cheeks.

'What are you going to do, Jew?' she asked.

'I'm going to find the son of a bitch who did this and feed him his balls,' I said angrily. The fury that developed in me overcame my misery.

'I figured you would when the police told me they couldn't find you after… after they found Mum and Dad in your…' she didn't finish, but I finished the sentences for her in my head. 'You are a strong determined man, Jew, but you have to let the police deal with this. Your state makes you incapable to search for justice by yourself.'

I was truly offended by this seemingly true statement. If I was truly blind, it was no debate that I could do nothing about my state of terrible affairs. But I wasn't blind and I was going to do something about everything I was currently immersed in. The police were looking for a blind man and they were looking for the wrong man. I wasn't going to make it easy for them.

'I want you to do something for me, Ruth. It's going to be difficult, but I want you to think hard and give me a list of all your Dad's associates – those he liked and hated. Send that list to me using my personal email address,' I said having a brainwave. 'Couple a list of your mother's as well. Old friends, new friends, and followers anything you think may help.'

'How are you going to use the internet?' Ruth said suspiciously. 'Do you have someone helping you?'

I had to remind myself that Ruth knew me blind. 'Let's say something like that,' I explained only in those words.

'Please let me help you, Jew,' she begged. Her voice had hesitant tremors in it.

'Help me by doing what I asked you,' I replied keeping my voice level. 'I have to go, Ruth. I'm sorry for everything.'

It was a long shot, but it was a start. If Ruth gave me those names, perhaps I could find something crucial to work on. I knew that my days were numbered and I knew I had to act fast as well. *Who could I make contact with, someone who could help me further?* The name *Choirmaster* germinated in my mind after thirty minutes.

Chapter Seven

Rumours were that the Choirmaster could make politicians sing. He could make them sing on both sides. Sing for their political campaigns and landslide elections or sing for their lives if they ever crossed him. He was infamous for his crude operations, his unlimited influence and his anonymity. To many, he was practically a ghost that haunted you if you placed your feet on the wrong sand.

Choirmaster was my uncle, the only biological relative I ever knew. I had seen him only twice and the last time we met, he had given me a secret phone number, which was to be used only at the most significant of times. The first time I had met him, I was sitting in a park, on the same bench Ms Parkinson had found me on, on the anniversary of her death. I carried out this ritual yearly and it made me remember where I had come from.

***

I was just sitting there, my mind set on how I was going to get the final approval to open my bank on the outskirts of the town from the stubborn legal officials. The fact that I was blind and worked to start a private bank, didn't appeal to them, especially when I had proposed to deal with foreign investments and money transfers from foreign clients. That final decision hindered my progress to the extent where the employees I had already recruited to work for me when the ribbon to my bank was cut were found reluctant to join me anymore. All of them had been banking me to come through and had risked many top-notch positions from their prior workplaces. I was seen to have destroyed healthy careers if my bank wasn't to be legally officiated to open.

Choirmaster had worn a velvet toped black hat, had a nicely trimmed moustache that matched the charcoal black colour of his sideburns. His taste of unbranded clothes had made him appear in a black overcoat. When he sat at the other end of the bench, a few meters from me, I had mistaken him for an undertaker for he was all in black.

'The white lady picked you up from that spot you are sitting,' Choirmaster suddenly said in an extraordinarily fine voice.

I was stunned so much that I looked at him forgetting that I was supposed to act blind. 'What did you say?' I erupted.

I couldn't see his eyes for, like mine, they were covered in shades. He sat looking straight.

'Jewel Dean Parkinson she named you. I wish my brother's whore could see what her son looks like now,' Choirmaster said looking as composed as nobody I had ever seen. 'She'd eat her fine ass to bits.'

It took me time to absorb and decode his words. When I had turned eighteen, Ms Parkinson had told me how she had found me. It had built so much hatred in me that I had vowed to make my mother pay one day. However, the hatred had taken a year to burn out after Ms Parkinson had made me take a vow to her trust. I had vowed that no matter what, if I ever got to come across my biological parents, I would treat them like family. It was a lot of bullshit, but I followed Ms Parkinson's wishes. As such, I had made sure that I would never come across my real parents to execute those wishes. That would save me from the fangs of betrayal.

Suddenly hearing someone talk about my mother stunned me, but it didn't resurrect any bad feelings I had for her.

'You are assuming that you are my father's brother,' I said imitating Choirmaster, looking straight ahead at a couple of children that were playing in the park.

'I'm not assuming, I am telling you who I am, son,' Choirmaster said.

'Why?' I asked.

'Because I think it's time we met. I've been watching you from a distance, son. You have grown well. I respect that, I do,' Choirmaster said. I sensed the truth in his voice and it had seared my heart. 'Well done, son.'

'Stop calling me that!' I hissed. 'After all these years, I can't believe you have the nerve.'

'You are my brother's son, Parkinson, and that's irreversible. It's not something you can change. I sometimes envy myself for having not reacted. I should have taken care of you, son,' Choirmaster continued to annoy me.

I felt like jumping at him. 'Taken care of me? What about the ones who dropped their pants to enjoy moments of ecstasy to produce me? What, weren't they stomach-clenched enough to face what they had created, an unwanted blind bun?' I said and yet I didn't raise my voice. The fury in my voice made me tremble restlessly. 'Where is this so-called brother of yours, the sperm donor?'

'Your father, my brother, was a weak spoiled man. He took over our father's family business at a rather tender age,' Choirmaster related the story to me. 'Father died – nobody was there to give him advice. He sold the business and shared the money with our fancy mother. They lived happily never after. Mother wanted grandchildren before she died and my brother chose to delay having children as long as he could. He spent most of his life spending his fortune, to a point he spent it all only to end up in debt with notorious individuals who lent him money to support his bad habits. He stole all of mother's money and paid some of his debts. Even after all this, all mother could cry about was wanting grandchildren.

In an effort to lessen his shame of stealing from her, he managed to get one of his girls pregnant – your mother. My brother couldn't face the reality that he was going to present our mother with a blind grandchild knowing how severely selective and sensitive mother was. He stole a grenade from my warehouse and blew himself up. After discovering that the father of her child was no longer there to provide her with easy dough, your mother left you on that spot you are sitting. I watched all this from that tree over there,' Choirmaster pointed to a huge Msasa tree that was rooted close to the pavements that led to and from the park. 'I could have killed her there and then after what I saw, but when that old lady took you, I let it go. I knew she would take care of you better than anyone else in the world.'

Choirmaster stood up and left leaving me all wet with questions and more confusion. I had learnt more about myself in a few minutes than I had done in more than twenty years. On the next day, my bank's foreign operations application was approved and I couldn't help feeling that my so-called uncle had played a major role for it to happen.

***

'What do you want from me? Name it and I'll provide,' Choirmaster's voice came from the other end of the line.

'I want you to provide me with information. Anything deep you can find on Mr and Mrs Tariro – not the general stuff anyone can google – and if anyone has a grudge against me that I don't know off,' I told him. I was sure this was going to be easy for him, so I piled up the needs and wants on his table. 'I also need you to get me all the police records, forensic, whatever that was developed from the murder scene. I also need, er…' I thought for a while. 'I need a laptop and some supply of food.'

Ironically, Choirmaster laughed. 'Why don't you let me look after you? You are blind, remember, you're easy to spot if you wish to go on this finding-out-who-framed-you thing, Parkinson.'

It suddenly occurred to me that my uncle didn't know of my way of ways. He surprisingly didn't or hadn't discovered that I could see. 'I've someone helping me, sir. I appreciate the offer anyway.'

'Okay, son, whatever you need. However, I need not tell you what kind of trouble you are in now. Everyone you get in touch with and who helps you will be treated the same by the police, worse off Division. If you feel that it is wise to do this solo or with whoever is helping you now, I hope you know what you are doing, son. Because if you get caught, you'll be found half-guilty before they even set you on trial,' Choirmaster explained to me what I already knew and I was annoyed to hear it coming from him.

I rested on my motel's bed and lay on it relaxing my muscles. 'I know,' was my simple response.

'How do I get these things to you?' he asked.

'I'll call you and provide you with a location,' I informed him.

I knew I had to find a safe place to hide. Motels were public facilities. I couldn't stay in them for more than two days without coming across someone who recognised part or the whole of me.

Choirmaster wished me luck before I hung up. If I asked the man to find a safe hideout for me, I was confident that he would deliver. He could find a place where I would live for years without the authorities ever getting a sniff of me. But a small voice inside me advised me that whatever I was going to or not discover was bigger than all of us, even the Choirmaster himself.

The next day was filled with less activity for it was a Sunday. I ordered for some food using the free delivery service. I sent my orders to five different outlets, different companies and different food. Every time the delivery boy or girl arrived with the food, I wore a towel around my head, put a toothbrush in my mouth with some soap over my face and after taking my shades off, opened the door. It was a very difficult act that required me to blink often for me to see, but it was a well carried out play. The delivery personnel went away without a hint of suspicion, possibly thinking of the motel guest who was pimping his face with a lady's beauty facial lotion and was being tormented by having the lotion make him blink a lot. The food was enough to last me for two days, the period I had planned to stay at the motel. I had no idea where I was going next, but I knew it would be close by and deserted as well.

Sunday's morning passed with me rewriting my plan down. By afternoon, I had filled a dozen pages with slightly the same content I had scribbled the first time. With the new developments after calling Ruth and Choirmaster, I had a better outline. My chain of progress was now based on what I was going to be provided with by Ruth and mostly the Choirmaster. An additional difference was that, proving myself innocent was going to involve a lot of scouting and guessing. Bad guesses were going to cost me, but they were unavoidable. I was going to make them one way or the other. I had no time for perfection.

I switched on the TV of the motel's room and I was met by the afternoon news. It was a coincidence I belched on. The brutal murders of the Tariros were amongst the top headlines. The photo of me and my dark glasses on appeared likewise and there was speculation that I had left the country. That assumption publicized me as a guilty sick bastard who had hired some goons to kill Ruth's parents after she refused to accept my marriage proposal. The stories were forever varied in quality from different broadcasts. One TV station even had a nickname for me. I was now DJ Park the deranged criminal-minded businessman.

The afternoon passed as I watched a movie. It was a romantic one and it transported my thoughts towards BJ. I spent not less than an hour hallucinating about her. *How was she living? Did she still believe I was innocent? Did she think of me or had Chris brewed up a magic formula to win her heart?* I thought of Fluffy and remembered our one-on-one pawing and throwing. I ended up laughing, but the laugh made me bitter for I knew that memories were past tense. I was living a present tense of a ruined life.

CHAPTER EIGHT

My first run of bad luck in my world of black luck greeted me that Monday. I had my hood on, planning to buy a cap the moment I got a chance, walking along Msasa Drive in Msasa. A few lodges there were up for instant accommodation and I was hoping to find one that didn't have any children or housewives around. I was searching for something a bit low budget, something concealed and private. During the walk, I came across some sort of shopping centre.

The site possessed quite a number of small shops, but what caught my attention was a restaurant that was part divided into an internet cafe. I found myself walking in and I was met by its emptiness. I walked over to where the internet cafe half was located and placed a five-dollar bill on the counter. A lady attendant didn't look up to me when she slipped the money from the counter to where she sat concealed by an arching establishment, which was the counter. I requested for two hours.

The official charge was a dollar for an hour. The wall clock showed that it was a little after eight – morning time – so my duration was to last until ten A.M. I needed only two hours of the time, since the network service tended to slow down as the day progressed. The lady handed back my change without even raising her head. Curiosity got the better of me as I peeped over the solid counter to see what was holding her attention so much that her head was stuck. My shades fell over and I cursed myself for being reckless. I wasn't doing much to avoid scrutiny by invading privacies.

Astonishingly, the lady picked up the glasses and placed them on the counter her head unmoved. Overcompensated by the brief luck, I murmured "thanks" and dashed away.

I found a deserted computer and logged onto the net. The first thing I did was to check my local assets online. As I had anticipated, they were all frozen. For someone who had much to lose and nothing to be surprised of anymore, it didn't bother me much. My priceless goal now was freedom and that was that. If need be, I had other assets secretly stashed in nearby foreign countries.

The shirt I wore was now sticky to my frequently sweaty body. However, it still possessed a whiff of BJ's perfume. My highly sensitive nose could smell the stench that was slowly developing from my feet. I hoped the people who were going to trickle in eventually to use the cafe didn't possess my kind of nose. I didn't want to get caught just because I had smelly feet. The thought made me smile, mainly as a remedy to keep me in some kind of balance.

I had chosen the computer that looked modern, overlooking a few chairs of the restaurant. The network was appealingly fast that I opened quite a number of pages at the same time, switching from one to the other during each page's loading process. I goggled for the businessman I was supposed to have murdered. I saw lots of stuff that proclaimed me as the country's number one criminal. Not much stuff was directed at Mr Tariro on the first page I saw. The next pages presented stuff I didn't think I knew, but stuff I felt I needed to know. I scrutinized the machine and was energized to discover that it had a Bluetooth facility that was compatible with my cellphone's Bluetooth platform. I copied and saved the information onto my phone to read later and unhurried.

As I browsed over the net, I suddenly came across a suspicious looking mail in my inbox. At first, I thought it was a virus of some sort or someone who knew my private email address and wanted to be funny regarding my abrupt infamous status.

It was written: *BANKING WITHOUT SIGHT.*

I opened it. I was practically stunned by what I saw. The mail had about eleven lines and I read each word with the pace of a snail. My mind was full of questions. *Was this a coincidence or did it have a significant meaning?* Then I caught the initials BJM at the end of the mail and I knew.

Barbara's mail was direct to the point. She wanted to help me in any way she could and the mentioning of her having told her brother the whole story made me panic. I suddenly began to sweat, peeping around as if I had felt someone pointing at me.

The cafe and restaurant had gradually filled up, but not too many people occupied the computers to surf the web. I read the mail repeatedly developing different thoughts with each read. Another thought came to me. *How did BJ know my private email address?*

A spam suddenly popped on the screen waking me up from my thousand thoughts. I remembered Barbara telling me that her brother was a computer scientist of some sort and guessed it to be the *"how"* she had got my private email address. If that was the real explanation then I assumed Barbara's big brother to be good at what he did because my email as a banker who was obsessed with privacy and security, it wasn't something one would acquire easily.

Deep in thought, I suddenly received a message after the command prompt window suddenly popped up. I was perplexed so much that I had to shake my head to get my neurons working. Someone was remotely accessing the computer I was working on. And with what was written on it, I knew that that someone knew that I was online to do that. A sudden fear flowed within me. My bone structure froze to ice. I read the message.

Dean, I am Mike Maya, Barbara's brother

I typed in:

What are you doing? Where are you and how do you know that I am currently online?

…and sent the message. I waited anxiously for an instant reply. It came and its popping on the screen nearly gave me a heart attack. I opened it.

I am here to help you Dean. I am on the fourth computer from the booth you are in and I know a little about computers

The message read, answering my question.

On the computer where… you are what? I thought. The chair I was sitting on moved aimlessly as I jerked. Anxiety tearing me apart, I turned my head slowly to see who sat in the fourth booth. I could partially make out the man for he was half covered by the booth. The man wore a black suit's jacket. He had his head set on the screen of his computer.

I shook my head again and looked back at my screen to see another message pop on.

Don't act like you know or recognise me. Somebody might be watching ready to make a move

I wondered to what extent BJ had told Mike about me. I typed in:

How did you find me?

He responded:

I put a tracer on your email addresses so that whenever you tried to use them, they would pinpoint your actual location. I had to divert my route to work to dash here in hope that I would find you

I typed in:

Why did you want to find me?

The answer was easy, but I wanted to know for sure.
He replied:

I promised B that I would find you, help and take you to her apartment where she claims you will be safe.

It surprised me a little, but I deemed that the two must have a very strong bond for Mike to reach such heights of wanting to help me for real. He could have just called the police and worse, that morning my head was worth five hundred thousand dollars.

When I had seen it on the news, it hadn't registered in my head. News nowadays meant a lot of rubbish aimed toward lies and more lies. I wondered if it was genuine or just an un-researched rumour. Mr Tariro's brothers had offered a reward for anybody who caught me or assisted the police in doing so.

The story had said that the person or persons who managed to catch the dangerous blind psychopath and his accomplices who had killed their brother and sister-in-law was going to be handed the money there and then without questions.

It was too much money and I suddenly realised it now with BJ's brother sitting a few meters offering to help me. Money was the motivator of all crap necessary or not. Everybody knew that.

Didn't this man in a suit want easy money?

'Mummy, mummy – the glasses man! Look, the glasses man!'

The voice was like a series of squeaks and it took me time to understand what was going on. I looked at where the squeaks had come from and saw a five-year-old girl pointing at me excitedly. She had her hair braided and tied by a red ribbon. Her chubby little face gleamed as she pointed a candy stick toward where I sat visible to one-half of the restaurant. Her mother looked up and her eyes and my closed ones behind the dark glasses locked. She rose up, grabbed little missy and screamed pointing at me.

My shocked attention swayed back at the computer screen in front of me. All the windows I had opened closed at once in a flash.

'Let's get the hell out of here!' Mike hissed rising from his station and he came up with a laptop bag that looked curiously similar to his sister's. He also wore black leather gloves. For the first time, I made him out. He looked immaculate and the features he inherited from the family gene pool made me fade doubts about him being Barbara's brother.

I rose and followed him, as many people looked around wildly, searching for the cause of the unrest. As we made for the door as fast as we could, two men who were having breakfast at a table near the window out-looking the restaurant's interior made me and were up in a dash. I pushed Mike out of the door and yelled at him to run. Mike ran and looked funny in his neatly cut formal attire and bag. I followed in his tracks with the two men behind us, five hundred grand floating in their heads.

The men did their best to shout out *"catch him!"* but it only seemed to confuse the onlookers more for they were caught in the action too fast to think.

My cellphone suddenly flew from my jacket's pocket and crashed onto the windshield of a car that was parked outside a pharmacy. It cracked and dropped to the ground after bouncing off the windshield's shiny surface creating a dent. I only managed to grab it and sprinted after Mike clasping it firmly.

An old lady was just opening her door from a Mazda 3 ready to do her shopping, a white handbag in one hand, and her car keys in another. I watched as Mike snatched the keys from her, pushed her toward the pavement's lawns and inserted himself into the car gesturing me to run quickly to occupy the other side. I did so without trying to think twice.

He swerved the car fiercely from the parking lot, I in the process of trying to get my seatbelt on. A brick was fired at my window and the window sagged inwards. I peered out to see who had had the nerve and saw that it was one of the men, a tall man with such bravado painted all over his dark face.

Mike reversed out to the left side of the parking lot and changed the gears with amazing agility. He stepped on the gas and, as he sped to leave the vast parking area, he hit a green Toyota on the rear side, destroying almost all of it. The Toyota's backlights exploded into the air spraying numerous coloured plastic and metal fragments to the car's windshield. I stared horrified at Mike, but his face was screwed for business. His whole concentration focused at what was going on with the car we had stolen.

Michael sped along the roads of Msasa negotiating the corners like a formula one Grand Prix driver. I took the time to gaze into the rear-view mirror and was weakened. A silver Mercedes was gaining in for the kill. I could espy the two men from the restaurant, Mr Bravado and Mr Drunk. The men had committed themselves into working hard for that five hundred gees and I trembled when I realised that such a lot of dough would prompt a lot to do anything to get it. People had even killed for far less.

The car chase brought many people from their houses, mostly young children and housewives for it was a working day. What most of them saw was the tail of our speeding cars.

The frustrating seconds passed before I succeeded in buckling myself up with the car's seatbelt. Mike had no seatbelt on or showed any signs of wanting it on. His focus was the gears and the road. Although I was drowned by fear of being involved in an accident than being caught if I survived one, I had to admit that Mike was one bloody devil on wheels.

Where was he going? Was he taking me to the police to claim the reward himself before the competitors caught up with us? What about the car? We had stolen an old lady's car and I hoped it wasn't taboo.

Suddenly, he clipped on his seat belt and before I knew what was happening, Mike smashed the car directly into the durawall of one house and airbags from the car bloomed. However, that didn't kill the car completely. I yelled out as Mike insanely destroyed another wall to enter into another house's yard. This time the car did die after a noisy shriek. I followed his lead for it was his party. We hastily exited from the car, most of my vision blurry at first. We were all shaken a bit, but we managed to stagger, climb and jump the other walling from the other house. We landed into a deserted street that led into a number of adjacent roads to three flat buildings. We ran towards one area and climbed up the stairs in a hurry. The path ended at the top of one of the flats where junk was kept. We chose a spot that gave us an aerial view and moulded ourselves in.

What I saw was so fascinating it made my heart beat much faster than what the run had done. The view gave us sight to the two houses that were imminent to the area where the flats were built. I could see what the car had done. It had bored through two parallel walls.

The owners were now up and about, shouting at the owners of the Mercedes who had cunningly used the gored up route in an attempt to catch *the blind man*. The owners wanted explanations and the two men kept on referring to the car we had left in the other house. We spent fifteen minutes cramped in our positions without saying a word to each other, watching. It was evident that the officials were going to arrive very soon. We made sure that nobody was lingering around looking for us before we circumspectly left the flat.

'You are one crazy person, man,' I was the first to talk as we walked along a street that led us from the flats and practically the hot zone.

Mike took off his tie smiling nervously and pulled out his cellphone. 'Thank me later,' he said.

He called someone as I scrutinised my phone. The screen was a mess and one SIM card had slipped off. Fortunately, it was the one registered in my name. I had no much use of it anyway. I knew the following days were going to be a lifetime experience. I was stolen away from the world as my mind contemplated on all possible endings to my story and possibly my life.

CHAPTER NINE

Barbara had picked us up on the edges of Msasa, using a company's car that had some kind of lingo I didn't see clearly, perhaps because of the state of total unrest that I was currently exposed in. The two had exchanged chat as I had sat in the back seat observing the tenderness of how they communicated. BJ had glanced at me twice during the ride as Mike told her what had happened.

If I was like the most wanted person in the world by now, I couldn't have been more surprised. I knew that that day evening's news was going to be something else. I had broken records and records in the world of crime. DJ Park was the most infamous person in the country.

After dropping us off at her apartment, BJ had left for work whilst Mike went back home to change and then for work. He knew he needed an extremely strong alibi if anybody had identified him in the craziness. A possibly strong alibi was work and he was intelligent enough to develop it into a steadfast one.

Left at the apartment, I tried to replay the furious action, but failed. Bits and pieces of memory were scattered all over my cognition and – amongst other scary notions – I was confident that my head was going to explode one way or the other. It was an endangered case. Fluffy sat on my lap, rather cuddled warmly, purring like we had been the best buddies. She did it for more than an hour before I suddenly smelt just how bad my skin was commuting to become and, after a moment of hesitation, I went to wash off my filth in Barbie's intriguing bathroom. I wore my old stinky clothes, but felt fresh.

BJ returned later that day. She came back famished from a day that she defined as slave labour at the office. She however had the amazing strength and nerve to give me a hug. Something about the way she snuggled into me, the way her arms locked around my neck and the way I could feel her heartbeat scared me into far away galaxies. She held me for a minute before letting me go. Her eyes searched for mine from the dark glasses and she smiled. I nervously smiled back.

'Hi, Dean,' she said with her exquisite voice.

'How are you, Barbie-J?' I said and my hand went up to brush away the few strands of her perfect black or brown hair smoothly from her face. An automatic reaction that even surprised me. Her face beamed with joy. I drew my hand back as quickly and as composed as I could.

'I've been better,' she said looking me over. 'We should find you some clothes. My shampoo smells alluring mixed with your fine short hair.'

I looked up at her and tried to mask a frown that ended up being a grin.

'I'm glad you finally made yourself at home, Dean,' she said making way to her bedroom, Fluffy on her heels.

I smiled and sat on the sofa, where I deemed I was going to crash for a long time.

Ten minutes later, she returned in pink sweatpants and a matching pink top that had a kitten braided on it. She looked amazing that I kept my eyes as open as possible so that I couldn't battle with the emotions that were crawling their way to my senses.

I fumbled uneasily with the TV's remote and switched the TV on.

BJ busied herself by preparing diner. She was over-talkative, reciting what Mike had told her. I confirmed the authenticity of the story and along the conversation, I learned quite a lot about the Mayas. Close wasn't the right word to use for they simply adored each other.

Mike and BJ had gone to the same schools and Mike had always been the big brother. No dude had dared messed around with BJ. High school had been more difficult because of BJ's unique looks. She was the cream of the crop and being the Big Brother then had had its stresses. I understood then why BJ had told Mike about me as well as my secret. I wondered if I could also confide in her more.

'So, Dean, how have you been coping since you walked out on me – leaving me locked in my own apartment?'

The question came and I knew it had been due anyway. I was ready for it and I told her my story. She was truly amused at the way I had stayed low until a kid had made me out.

'How do you plan on getting all that information?' she asked, very much knowing my only answer.

'I've my own secret sources,' I told her.

She grinned at me and began arranging the dishes to serve. 'Who, anybody I know?'

'Have you ever heard of Choirmaster?' I asked her in a teasing tone.

Almost everybody had heard of the Choirmaster and I bet that if BJ somehow knew who I was before we had met ninety-eight per cent of the chances were that she knew of my uncle. Choirmaster was one of the most controversial ghosts in the country – he seemed mythical.

'Choirmaster as in *the Choirmaster?*' BJ's mouth was wide open with disbelief. She stared at me stunned.

'Yes,' I said simply.

'You know the Choirmaster, Dean?' her eyes bored into me. 'He is like the… er – Dean, I don't believe you.'

I smiled and gladly accepted the plate of pasta and mince she held out for me. She threw a fork at me as if annoyed by what I had just told her.

'I don't believe you,' she said again.

'I know, nobody would,' I said tucking in BJ's lovely dinner. 'He is my best source now and possibly the only person who can get me out of this shit.'

BJ came to sit on the sofa and snuggled closer to me, gradually sitting with her leg on the sofa, a position she was fond of. I couldn't help noticing that she wanted to be as intimately close to me as she could get. I pressed myself to the shoulder of the sofa, scared of her closeness. She ate her meal, her eyes glued on me. My gaze was fixed to what I was eating.

'You are serious?' she said. 'Is he even real or a person, but a group of people with so much power?'

'Why would I lie about that, Barbie?' I said firmly with a confident tone. 'He is a real person. You yourself should know that knowing the Choirmaster is just as dangerous as being the Choirmaster himself.'

BJ giggled and pinned her fork into her pasta. She rolled the pasta on the fork and plunged it into her mouth. Her chewing was combined with a teasing smile.

'You live a pretty exciting life, Dean,' she said after swallowing. 'How do you know the Choirmaster? You are a businessman, but not that big.'

I laughed and chocked in the process. 'Choirmaster happens to be my biological uncle,' I told her and was excited by her reaction. She looked angelic in confusion and taste. I smiled and it felt good.

The sudden flash of the daily news suddenly wiped that smile. Thanks to Mike, I was the news. It was the moment of convoluted stories. The newscast was set at the location where Mike had transformed fiction into reality. The police officials were all over the scene, detectives detecting shit and police interrogating the two men who had pursued us. The owners of the houses we had bored walls of were very animated. They related that they had heard some kind of chaos when Mike had run the disintegrated Mazda into the walls. The TV showed just how messed up the car was. It was hard to imagine anybody having survived without any scratches from the commotion.

The main question was how could someone blind drive a car and manage to evade capture? The introduction of a serious accomplice was painted into the picture. Luckily for us, nobody had made out who my accomplice was or yet. I knew that BJ's brother was very anxious now. If anyone had identified what he looked like, we would probably be in the same shit. My advantage in such an ironic situation was that I was known as blind. Mike would automatically become the doer or my hired doer. The authorities were now looking for an individual helping a blind man. Sarcastically minded, I wished them luck.

The reward money had insanely been toped up to a million bucks. More people would surely make it their business to find me now. It was really a tempting offer that I second-trusted the only two people who knew where I was. A million dollars was fortune. The Tariro brothers must have really been pissed to stake me out like that.

'Wow, Dean, your head is now worth a mill,' BJ stood up and, finding something to do with her hands to avoid them from showing just how nervous she was now, she carried our plates to the kitchen.

'Yeah,' I said, my tone prompting her to continue. *Was she going to betray and cash me in?* I thought, my heart racing.

'It's funny that,' she giggled coming back to sit much closer to me. I could smell her skin and breath. I was dizzy for a while intoxicated by the odour, 'they would put a price tag on you. They must have so much money these people. A million dollars – seriously?'

'Funny?' I breathed heavily.

'Yeah, it's like you are some world terrorist or something. If they had any idea that that head possessed eyes that could see with their lids closed and couldn't whilst open, believe me, Dean, your supposed crimes will simply be a bedtime story.'

I found the humour in her voice charming. It was true. My phenomena secret was worth international fame. I wondered if that was the reason why BJ and her brother were helping me, keeping me away from the hands of the authorities.

'Why are you so interested in me to help me?' I asked, curiosity getting the better of me. A lot of things weren't making sense at all.

Barbara-Jean narrowed her eyes at me and gave me a look that made my heart lean back from its position, sending tingling impulses to my feet and ears. Her left leg crooked on the sofa, sitting on it – she mobilised towards me in what appeared to me as slow motion. Her right hand supported her weight as she bent over towards me, her knees now pivoting her back on the sofa. She let her weight fall down on me and perfectly landed her lips on my terrified mouth.

At first, her moves shocked me totally, but as she kissed me passionately, her tongue mischievously rolling on mine, I melted like butter on a scorching day. I felt her amazing body rest on top of mine, forcing me to change from my sitting position to recline on the sofa. Some of her hair fell from the back tickling my face. The world seemed to disappear from us as we exchanged passion. I swear that I remember floating like a cloud, in an indescribable feeling.

Wickedly, thoughts were catapulted back towards me like a train slamming in my face. I controlled myself and slowly pushed BJ off me.

'That's why I am helping you, Dean, that's why,' BJ said in a voice that was like a melody of stammer.

She sat back and folded her arms, her back resting at the opposite arm of the sofa, her eyes fixed at me. I could see them sparkle as her mouth screwed a satisfied smile into a grin.

'So you could kiss me?' I teased her, making sure that she wasn't going to try it again abruptly. If she did, I was ready to flee because I knew that this time it wouldn't end that way. I already possessed dangerous feelings for this lady and mocking them wasn't a wise idea.

BJ didn't answer, but smiled in response. The knock on the door woke us. BJ dashed toward it and peeped through the peephole. Her face beamed with an expression of joy. I guessed correctly, when she didn't hesitate to open the door, an idea of who it was.

Mike and I shook hands at half-seven that evening. He had the air of unbelievable respect toward me. I tried to guess why, but couldn't come up with an answer – a clear one that was.

'You made the news, Dean,' Mike said amiably, unpacking his laptop. Fluffy fussed around him as she did with her mistress.

'No, Mike, we made the news,' I said intrigued by the amount of small gadgets he produced from his bag. Some of the stuff I could only guess. 'Frankly, I did nothing, but hold onto your tail.'

Mike and his sister laughed. It was a lovely sound to hear, especially for a person who had faced the hell I was in.

'I've some interesting finds on my search,' Mike said switching on the laptop. It had an operating system I had never seen or heard of before. 'You were right, Bee. This is messed up big time.'

I was left out a bit as they exchanged mysterious talk.

'Hey, what are you two talking about?' I finally stopped them.

Mike punched a few keys and turned around to face me as I was now pacing behind the sofa. BJ was kneeling with one leg on the sofa, her arm on Mike's shoulder as her eyes were fixed to the laptop's screen.

'*Silver Bond Market Bank* has three accounts belonging to Mrs Tariro. All held USD$7 000 0000 each before her death.'

'Excuse me – did you say Mrs Tariro as in the wife of Mr Tariro, the business tycoon, the one I'm suspected to have butchered?' I asked bewildered.

'Yes, Dean, that Mrs Tariro,' Mike confirmed, showing me the transaction on the screen running his finger along them. 'Here is the date the accounts were opened. They were opened on the same date. And here, when they were closed after all the money was transferred to an offshore account. All at the same date, the day after her death. Very queer indeed, right?'

I shook my head and blinked twice, shook my head again and

breathed. 'Who transferred the money?' I said, barely audible.

Mike punched a few buttons and paused from pressing *Enter* then punched it. He did a double a double take.

'Here it claims that the President of the bank transferred the money,' he said a bit stunned.

I stood straight and felt my knees buckle a little. I was the President of Silver Bond Market Bank. The deeper these things penetrated, the more shit that we dug, the more stuck I was in it.

I swore hard and looked away from the two shocked Mayas.

Chapter Ten

I didn't ask how he was doing it, but Mike hacked into my bank's network as if it was an unprotected Pentium II computer. He showed us quite a lot of stuff, but he unbelievably failed to decode how Mrs Tariro had had three different bank accounts holding so much money at Silver Bond Market Bank and why they had suddenly been closed after her murder. The fact that I was supposed to be the one who had transferred the money had me in bliss of disorganisation.

We discussed about the issue until eleven when Mike's wife called him and he had to leave. He promised to stay in touch on the next day and advised me to stay put at BJ's house. I asked BJ for the physical city's map before she went to bed. Luckily, she had one. It took me a while to get it from her for she demanded answers of why I needed it.

I couldn't tell her that I was currently planning to meet my uncle. Although she now knew that I was related to Choirmaster, that didn't give her the privilege to know who he was for real. Choirmaster was a man who wealthily prized his privacy. I didn't want in any way to violate it. He was my uncle, but he was also the Choirmaster. Abusing my familiarity with him by telling people, trusted or not, who he genuinely was would have been utter foolishness.

BJ left me for bed fuming, claiming that I was truly naive not to trust her enough to give her at least a clue on why I wanted her map. I worked on the map until one in the morning when my stressed body gave in to fatigue. The spot I had spent a difficult time selecting didn't appeal much to me, but with my state of mind and anatomy, it was the best secretive spot I could find. After the most incredible day I had survived to remember, I only wondered how my uncle was going to react. My infamous reputation was escalating to unbelievable heights as each day progressed.

I searched for my phone and later realised what had happened to it. I moaned in frustration as I thought of all the data that was in it. *How was I to call the Choirmaster?* My thoughts later came across BJ. She had a phone, in fact two. I searched the dining room, the kitchen and the sitting room, which was of course the dining room or a combination of both, and my heart pulsated with each object I found which had the shape of a cellphone. Thirty minutes ended up in disappointment. The only way I could use BJ's phone was asking for one and be tormented with numerous questions.

The alternative was just to steal one as she was sleeping now. Without thinking much, I tiptoed to her bedroom and prayed that she wasn't one of those people who locked their rooms at night in fear of whatever they thought would happen to them as far as the bedroom was concerned. It was unlocked.

My heart beat faster as I slowly opened her door. Luckily, her light was still on. Fluffy raised her ear, then opened one eye and saw me. She went back to sleep unconcerned. Her madam was snuggled in nicely. She wore a hairnet and, amusingly, night blinds. *Why not just switch off your lights?* I mocked in thought.

For a while, as I peeped through her door, I almost forgot why I was doing it as her face – peaceful in sleep – hypnotized me that I couldn't look away. My thoughts wavered in many dimensions. Moments later, I found myself standing in front of her bed, my gaze fixed on her.

The long run of my visions ultimately halted after I don't know how long and mercilessly snatched me back to reality. I looked for what I was looking for and found the two phones on her bed's sideboard surface. They were both high tech gadgets and it took me a few seconds to choose the appropriate one.

I picked the phone I thought I could operate easily after a few trials of evaluating and the choice was made for me as I picked the other one, which had no passcode on it.

I left the room as slow as possibly quiet as I could. I breathed when I closed the door behind me and started to dial my uncle's private number from memory. About to let the call go, I stopped, paused, my thumb on the call icon and cancelled the transaction.

I slipped the back of the phone open and removed the battery. I inserted my SIM card and was amazed to discover that the phone could accommodate four SIM cards.

The sister of a computer whiz, I thought grinning.

I made sure that my SIM was solo in the phone before reassembling it. I called Choirmaster.

'Dean, my boy,' Choirmaster said a lot of humour in his voice. 'You are quite active for a blind person.'

I let him rumble on about the day. As expected, he had done the math and I was a bit anxious. *Did he know who had helped me out?* I thought. He was the kind of man who could easily discover such things if he wanted to.

'Did you get what I asked for, sir?' I asked him.

'Whenever you need the info, please tell me where and when,' he replied. 'You'll be fascinated by what I found out, son.'

What could be more fascinating than what Mike had discovered? I hoped it wasn't more putrid.

I gave him my desired location of meet. He told me that he would personally deliver the compiled information.

Could I trust him? I thought.

A million dollars was a lot of money enough to betray family. Choirmaster could just sell me out and be a sizzling currency rider.

'Meet me at eight or let's say ten P.M. today, sir,' I said my mind far ahead.

'Be careful, son.' Were his last words.

I thought a lot about how the meet I had arranged was going to occur. *Should I send someone else?* I thought.

Sending someone would mean I would be putting the Choirmaster's identity at risk. Whoever was going to be the person, they were going to come face to face with my uncle. If I was to send someone, it had to be either BJ or Mike. My uncle was expecting to see me at ten that evening and letting someone else do the meeting for me was going to be to an extent an insult.

'Very creepy.'

BJ's voice made me leap from the sofa. My glasses fell and I stared at her, my heart beating like a drum. I looked like someone who was praying standing with my eyes closed. *What had she heard?*

Her face was configured with a frown. I saw anger and a lot of things in her eyes. 'What's going on, Dean?' she said with the voice of someone who was just woken up.

'I'm sorry, I had to use a phone so I borrowed yours,' I said simply.

'Calling who at one in the morning?' she frowned more.

'My uncle,' I didn't deceive her. 'I needed his help on something.'

BJ shrugged. 'Do you care to let me in on your plan, Dean?' she asked.

'There is no plan you don't know,' I said firmly. 'What did you hear?' I asked, seeing the doubt on her face.

'Enough to know that you'll be somewhere today at ten P.M. to meet...' she paused and breathed, '... the Choirmaster. Isn't that a plan, Dean?'

I looked like an idiot, dumbfound. *How the hell had she heard all that without me sensing her presence?* I cursed inwardly.

'How about giving me some benefit of doubt, Dean,' she shrieked waving her hands in the air. 'Don't I deserve that much?'

She left me feeling extremely pale. The slam of her door made me jump. I fumbled with her phone and lay on the sofa, my sofa, I didn't know for long. I slept after an hour of thoughts.

The smell of toast woke me up and I had a headache. I rose slowly from the sofa and replayed my sordid days in my mind. Many minutes passed as I sat thinking. I took the remote from a nearby stool and flicked the TV on. As if by coincidence, I was received by the news. It was a couple of minutes after seven morning time. My head was still a cool million worth to capture. The city was said to be in a frenzy of unrest.

Some were looking out for a notorious killer who was blind and had an accomplice. My accomplice was still a mystery although the police had tried hard to identify Mike. That was good news for me.

Suddenly, feeling thirsty, I visited the kitchen. Barbara looked up at me once as I entered. She refocused her attention to her breakfast ready to leave for work. Gazing at her laptop bag on the kitchen table, I was surprised that by now I still didn't know her type of trade. It was an embarrassing realisation really.

'Are you an IT expert as well?' I said, wondering if our early morning's heated discussion was still occupying her conscience.

She stared at me with dead serious eyes. I blushed as I saw the apprehension in her eyes. Fortunately, she couldn't see what my eyes had in them. They were filled with doubt.

'No, I'm a Finance Supervisor with PriceWaterhouse,' she replied and sipped some hot coffee. Her voice remained calm as if nothing was amiss.

Then I understood how she had known who I was long before we had met. PriceWaterhouseCoopers and Silver Bond Market Bank had been involved in quite a number of businesses together.

I had a great working relation with the firm.

'Oh, I see,' I finally said.

'Glad to hear that,' Barbara said. 'Here, take it,' she said and I saw her producing a cellphone I hadn't seen before. She handed it up to me and gestured impatiently at me to take it.

I took the phone and it looked new. 'Er –'

'Don't ask,' she cut me. 'I've got many of those. At least now, you don't have any excuses to sneak up into my room. Mike promised to bring a laptop for you to use some time today.'

Silence stole the air for a few seconds before I said something.

'Thank you, Barbara. I don't know what I can ever do to repay you,' I thanked her.

'I know what you can do, Dean,' she said and advanced up to me. I backed away slightly not sure what she had in mind. She looked devastatingly ravishing with a frown on. 'You can start trusting me. I know who your uncle is and I know that telling someone about him is very dangerous. But remember, Dean, as long as you are on the run and labelled guilty, we are now all in danger. You need to believe in me just as I do in you, Dean. See you.'

She placed her breakfast plates in the sink, grabbed for her laptop bag and left without saying goodbye. I felt rotten inside, as if some part of me was lost.

I owed my success in eluding the officials to the Mayas. No matter how grateful I was, I was still confused. *Why would these two people who had been living practically good untainted lives go out of themselves to help someone like me and someone who faced the awesome complications I was? Was I missing something else here?* I was undeniably the most wanted man in the country with a million-dollar tag around my neck. *Who would desire to become part of that by choice?*

I thought that it was maybe an endless bad dream, but then ended up feeling as if that dream was a tramp stamp preaching about my woos of an unhealthy life.

CHAPTER ELEVEN

As he had promised, Mike didn't turn up that day. It had me in all anxious moods. I began to panic at one time, assuming that perhaps he had developed cold feet. The day passed with me lazing on the sofa, watching the TV. The movies I watched were romantic comedies and they did somehow sooth me into a calm state. For that moment in time, life was lovely, but only for that brief time. The aftermath was drenching. The problems returned to my recognition with full force, I nearly suffocated.

I gazed at the wall clock and a few hours were pending. The Choirmaster was going to meet me at ten at my specified rendezvous. I had to leave BJ's apartment at eight.

My thoughts turned to BJ's cat as she snuggled on the sofa close to me. Since I fed her with lots of milk and fish fingers during the time we were together, I was now her favourite buddy.

The opening of the front door woke me up from my thoughts. Barbara entered looking a bit excited. I heard the screeches of car tires outside and did the math. Someone was living the site in a hurry. The look on BJ's face was that which involved the struggle of two expressions – a smile and a frown.

'Good evening, how is Chris?' I asked unexpectedly, as Fluffy dashed toward her mistress.

BJ glared at me, smiled shyly. 'How did you know?'

I did frown, not particularly clear of why I was doing it. I was wondering just how the jerk of a Chris had succeeded in making BJ be unsure of her facial expressions and, mostly, bring her home.

'Guessed,' I responded simply, not trying to sound like the way I was feeling.

Barbara shrugged and I noticed that she had an extra bag. It had the makings of a laptop carrier. 'Here, Mike passed by my workplace,' she said giving me the bag.

I took it and immediately opened it. The machine inside was

a high tech computer that included lots of I didn't know what accessories. Barbara left me checking it out.

The laptop was composed of a custom-made operating system and was configured to access the internet just by plugging in a customised wireless modem. The modem was also amongst the particulars. I inserted it in the network slot that was designed at the edge of the machine.

I logged on and went straight to check my mail. I was surprised when I saw the mail I had requested, but forgotten all about. It was an email from Ruth. I took my time opening it, wondering what I was going to find.

Ruth's mail was very touching that I nearly produced tears. She was very concerned about me and she endlessly advised me to turn myself in before someone tried to catch me only to end up hurting me. As I had requested from her, she had provided me with a list of her deceased parents' associates.

Barbara caught me immersed in the mail and I didn't know she was behind me until she said, *"I care for you, Jew, you know I do."*

I jumped, looking back at her standing behind the sofa. BJ had just read part of the mail aloud and, stunned as I was, I knew she had read that part out because it was something that had caught her unawares. If she hadn't caught me reading that mail, I bet I could have never showed it to her. The grin on her face made me silly. I closed the window to something else on the screen.

'What?' BJ said innocently – if not dryly.

'Nothing,' I said, opening more windows on the laptop in an effort to cover my nervousness.

'Who was that from?' BJ asked, not letting me off the hook.

I shrugged helplessly. 'A friend called Ruth,' I told her who Ruth was and she gaped noisily behind me.

'She must really care for you to believe that you are innocent when you are actually accused of killing her parents,' BJ pointed out. I sensed some unrest in her tone.

'She does and we have deep feelings for each other that I myself can't even seem to understand,' I said subconsciously, my attention focused on the computer.

I later realised what I had said when no answer came and the water started running from the kitchen. I looked back to see nobody. She had departed for the kitchen. *Had I said something she didn't want to hear?* I quizzed over it. I suddenly remembered the way she had kissed me not many hours ago and cringed. Women were very transparent when it came to the way they reacted emotionally. More fabulous or not, BJ was still a woman. I gave her her space and worked on the info Ruth had sent me.

Most of the names Ruth had sent me were vague to me. I barely knew ninety percent of them. The people the Tariros had associated with were truly high-class oldies. I only knew some of them by reputation and I had never set eyes on them. I couldn't link any of them to murder and deranged minds.

With that, I thought of my meeting with Choirmaster, which was drawing near by the minute. Perhaps he was going to give me some real info as he had promised. I was behind the action line and I needed to act fast. The days were flying and my fugitive status wasn't getting any better just as I had nothing to contemplate and show to prove my innocence.

The news about me on the TV that day were pretty hilarious in a way. There was so much talk about where I was seen or not seen, who was helping me and who was going to catch me. It was all speculation for nobody was even close to guessing where I was hiding.

Barbara prepared dinner early that day and I guessed, with what she was wearing, that she had made up her mind to let me do the meet solo, as I desired.

'I thought you were going to make a fuss about coming along,' I teased her.

She smiled faintly for someone who often had a cheerful face on.

'I thought you didn't want me to come,' she said.

'I can't risk –' I said.

'– your life?' she cut me off and finished the sentence for me. 'Thanks for caring that much, Dean.'

I glanced at her and noticed her sudden unease. I guessed that it had a lot to do with my mail from Ruth. 'I may not come back tonight,' I dropped the bomb to her awareness.

She jerked, stunned by the abrupt announcement. 'What?' she cried, her plate and fork to the table.

I wished I hadn't been so egocentric to tell her. I could have done it without her knowing. It would have been much safer then.

'I'm sorry. I meant to tell you after –'

'After what, Dean?' BJ's voice was cold as ice. 'Where are you going to hide, ha? Rent a string of motels in foolish hopes of not getting caught? Remember that you are worth a million dollars caught. Everyone has their eyes open now for God's sake, Dean.'

'I know, BJ,' I told her, 'but Choirmaster can make me disappear off the radar with ease.'

She shrugged and folded her hands frowning. 'So you trust the Choirmaster more than Mike and me?' she seethed.

"...after all that we have done for you," concluded in my head. She didn't say it, but I knew she wanted to. Her brother was the main reason I wasn't caught by now. Not acknowledging that fact was like spitting on their faces.

'I trust you both and I care for you both,' I said in a soft tone meant to calm her. 'That's why I think I need to go underground until all this mess is over, if ever. Staying here and getting your priceless help only makes you more vulnerable to risk. I cannot allow it.'

BJ looked pale and tears welled up in her eyes. It was so embarrassing. She wasn't crying, but she looked miserably sad.

'I don't know how to tell you this, Dean,' she chocked the words.

I gazed at her with new eyes, curious. 'What?'

'I am pregnant,' she said staring on the floor.

'What?' I jumped to my feet.

Fluffy looked up at me unnerved for a while, staring from her mistress to a shocked me.

'I know it's yours,' Barbara informed me still eyes on the ground.

Time seemed to pause, and then I laughed frantically. 'You must be kidding me,' I said amused.

More tears crawled from BJ's eyes. *Was she serious?* I thought.

'I am serious, Dean. I am pregnant and I am sure that the baby is yours,' she sniffed, as if she had read my mind.

Now what is this? I thought a bit apprehensively.

'What are you playing at, BJ?' I said, my tone with some humour. 'You aren't pregnant – you don't look pregnant at all.'

When she looked up at me, I felt my heart collapse. No matter how much it didn't make any sense, the look in her eyes told me that she wasn't joking around. I knew that she was pregnant, but by whom was the question.

'You don't remember, do you, Dean?' she scared the hell out of me. She had a serious expression.

'Remember? What the bloody hell are you talking about?' I said, my head rocking from side to side.

It took her a while to respond. 'The party, the night we first met,' she said, sobbing a little.

'I don't get you, Barbara – we didn't first meet at a party,' I said confused to the soul.

'Mike warned me about this, I should have listened,' she totally lost me.

I shook my head to clear my mind before thinking again. 'Warned you about getting pregnant or what? Seriously, BJ, what are you on about?' I asked standing upright.

'He warned me that the people who took you must have caused you to... *purposeful amnesia,*' Barbara said, looking up at me. 'And I see that you don't remember a thing. We met two months ago before you vanished.'

I only stared at her and listened, thinking that she was playing with my head so that I wouldn't leave her after accepting the help my uncle was going to offer that night.

'When I saw you in the street that night, I just thought you didn't remember me,' she continued as I gaped. 'Then the news that you,' she continued as I gaped. 'Then the news that you had killed the Tariros and all made me think otherwise. Mike did some digging and told me that you had been missing for a long time.'

'Are you out of your mind, BJ?' I giggled sarcastically, staring at her stunned.

'No, Dean, sit down and listen!' she said firmly. I found myself automatically obeying. 'You can't tell me that what you feel for me is new. It isn't and the first time we laid eyes at each other on that evening, I knew that you were special. After all, I lost my virginity to you days later. I thought –'

'You what?'

'I thought that your memory would resurface when we kissed, unfortunately it didn't. I'm now carrying your child and you better believe it.'

The next hour passed with her telling me what she knew. Although I tried hard not to believe her, some of the things she said made sense because they answered quite a number of questions. I suddenly understood why of all people Barbara and Mike were protecting me and believed in my innocence. With that, I didn't believe in myself so much after Barbara's revelations. I had lost about two months of my memory. And if I didn't remember anything that had happened to me for the past few months, how was I to be confident that I hadn't been the one who killed the Tariros? As Barbara finished her tale, she left to get some aspirin. I called Mrs Maguma and what I discovered made me aware that the tide was just rising.

CHAPTER TWELVE

The corner in which I hid was dark enough to blend with my dark clothing. It was a peaceful night that smelt of an indefinable aroma. Wednesday being the day, the town was jam-packed with fun lovers who took the night pleasures at will.

Chilling in the corner with my hood on, Barbara's story replayed repeatedly in my head so many times that I almost reached a point of feeling nauseated. The truth was that there was no reason why Barbara would cook up such an incredible lie and that made her story no lie. However, something didn't check up. I had called Mrs Maguma and the way she had acted had left me bewildered.

Barbara was telling me that I had been MIA for two months. Mrs Maguma was acting as if I hadn't been missing for a single minute before the murders. That scared the wits out of me. Mrs Maguma was still adamant on my current stroll in the world of crime. She had updated me that Division had left someone to watch the house 24/7 just in case I decided to pop in and get a fresh pair of socks.

Choirmaster arrived at the rendezvous of my choosing exactly on the gong. He wore a long dark overcoat and his famous hat celebrated his head. From my position, I made sure that he was alone before I thought of approaching him.

After fifteen anxious minutes, I walked over.

'Dean, my boy,' he greeted me warmly.

'Uncle,' I said shaking hands with him. To me, he hadn't changed a bit since we had last seen each other. However, there were some stains of worry in his clever eyes.

'It's good to see that you are well, son,' he said cheerfully. 'How have you been with this entire fracas?'

'As you can see, I'm very good,' I replied ironically. 'Is that the info?' I pointed at a small briefcase he was carrying.

'You aren't messing around, are you?' Choirmaster smiled at my directness. 'Everything you asked for.'

'Thank you, sir, I appreciate it very much,' I shook his hand once more.

'I'd do anything to help you, son, you know that,' he said.

I hesitated for a while. This was the part where I was supposed to ask for more help as in a place to lay low whilst I sorted my business out. 'Sir, can I ask you something?'

'Shoot, son,' he said waiting.

I knew I had to find out and this was the person who could help me more than none. 'Where have I been for the past two months?'

Choirmaster was practically stunned for the first time. He stared at me for a while.

'How did you know?' he asked curiously.

'Know about what?' I didn't say anything to lead him on.

'You have been missing for a while, son. Nobody knew where you were after the party,' he said shaking his head. 'I searched for you with no success at all. When you called me that night, to tell me what had happened, I figured that they had *paid* you.'

'Paid me?' I asked astound.

'*Purposeful Amnesia Integration Design*,' he explained. Hearing the words from him made the hopes that I had in BJ's tale being biased fade away. 'Your memory was tampered with so that you couldn't remember anything from the time you were abducted to the day you woke up drenched in blood in your office. How did you find out, do you have your memory back?' he asked eagerly.

I shook my head to his disappointment. 'I don't remember shit.'

'Many people were worried when you disappeared, Ms Ruth Tariro the most. She did all she could to find you, until, well…' the Choirmaster looked at a distance. 'Her parents' bodies were found. Rumours were circulating that you had disappeared after stealing some money from your bank, especially after that party.'

'Were you at this party – what was the party for?' I said, not even conspicuous of my edgy voice.

Uncle nodded and placed his hands in his overcoat's pockets. 'It was one of those major events. It was the celebration party of the opening of Silver Bond Market Bank's third and biggest branch in the country in collaboration with *Makota and Brown Chartered Associates*, two weeks after the opening ceremony – a lot of money involved there.'

I absorbed in each word he said as if it was special water from a prophet. 'Was I with someone?'

The grin he gave me prepared me for what was coming. 'Many assumed you would appear with a gay partner. Most were shocked when that most beautiful young lady at the event had the nerve to approach you. You see, many joked on the fact that she was wasting her beauty on blind eyes, what good was that? I discovered something very interesting that day, son. I discovered that you could very much make her perfect features out as the rest of us. I believe she must have been the Angel that restored or, let's say, gave you sight.'

'Do you know who she was?' I asked my heart beating faster.

'How can I not?' Choirmaster said swaggeringly. 'After you vanished, she was amongst the first people I had checked. I also admit that Miss Maya isn't the kind of human being a straight man like myself can easily forget. I discovered that you knew her before the meeting. I discovered you two met and became familiar when the company she works for did the audits or finances for your bank before the third branch was opened. I guess something between you two clicked.'

I agreed with his point of view inwardly – the attraction to BJ part. *Who could blame me for having intense feelings for the woman if the Choirmaster of all people acknowledged her unique appearance?* His explanation of how I knew BJ made what BJ had briefly told me make sense, though I couldn't remember it. My situation was getting complicated with each minute.

'Do you remember her now?' he asked, eyeing me curiously.

I didn't think twice and I told him. There was no point in hiding this from him for he was like my special aid now.

'Good gracious,' Choirmaster said. 'I could have never guessed it to be so multifarious.'

'It gets more complex,' I said, not making reservations. 'She claims she is pregnant – with my kid.'

That knocked the sense from the old man. He looked more surprised than I had been, perhaps because I had been too confused then.

'You serious?' he asked, wondering if he had heard me correctly the first time.

I told him about what BJ had said and how she had said it.

For a while, I thought he was going to claim that she was biased. Instead, he reasoned with the logic. 'She doesn't want her baby to be born fatherless – I understand it all now. Even her brother risked his life to save you for his sister and – nephew or niece, wow!'

It really did sound like some kind of craziness, but the degree of its authenticity was still undetermined.

'What do you suggest, sir?' I searched for a way out.

Choirmaster put a hand on his chin and caressed it slowly with his thumb in thought. 'I can hide you better than nobody can, but Miss Maya will not approve of it. Staying with her will put her and the future baby at risk also. Whoever set you up has motive. Who knows if they will succeed in what they want. What I suggest, son, is…' he paused for a few seconds. '... that you let me hide you, only after you see Miss Maya and explain what you plan to do.'

The news BJ had shot at me before I had left her apartment had surely made her assume that I wasn't going to return there. *How foolish of me to have had slept with her to give her such a burden,* I chastised myself angrily.

Was BJ going to produce another *see-with-your-eyelids closed* toddler? *Was the baby really mine?* Of course, it must have been for the Mayas to go to the ends of sanity making sure I wasn't caught.

'Meet me at the park on the end of 8th Avenue at midnight today. I'll pick you up for the safe house,' Choirmaster said in a tone that meant that our meeting was over.

I hurried back to BJ's apartment as fast as I could without being spotted. The briefcase was light enough to avoid hindering my movements, but it was unnecessary baggage. I could have just given it to my uncle since I was going to meet him not far from then.

I first saw the fire from a distance. Approaching the site, I nearly fainted as I witnessed that the whole building was smoking in fire at varied angles. The fire fighters were hot in a furious battle against the deadly flames. Spectators and some of the building's residence owners were anxiously standing behind a barricade the police had created to prevent them from getting close to the horrifying scene. Cracks and explosions followed by screams filled the air frequently. I looked around frantically searching for BJ. I couldn't find her.

Had she got out safe, had she left the building?

I was numb with shock. The wing where BJ's apartment had been was in smoke, not yet consumed by the flames. I don't know what got over me, but I sneaked through the security and used the fire escape door to enter the burning building. I fought through the smoke and developing flames towards BJ's apartment. I knew that I was taking a huge risk. There was more than ninety percent that the building would collapse on me and I would be burnt alive. BJ might be safe after all, outside, but I wasn't going to take that chance. I had to be sure with no doubt. I reached the apartment door in a matter of seconds. It was closed.

I opened the door with a huff and I was met by a gunshot. The first bullet missed my head by centimetres, but the next caught me clean on the shoulder. My back slammed against the wall from the impact. I rolled down the stairs, my head wheezing, and the pain excruciating.

More gunshots missed me at the base of the stairs and I managed to heave myself up and staggered for survival. I heard footsteps behind me and started to run despite all the pain I was suffering. Two more gunshots clipped off the walls close to piercing me. Now in full force, the fire seemed so life threatening and loud.

I miraculously exited the building and I don't know how many meters I ran toward the crowd before I blacked out.

Chapter Thirteen

What I felt first was the throbbing of my weak pulse. As weak as it was, I could feel that the pain that was going to come soon was going to be blinding.

My eyelids were opened, so I couldn't see anything. I closed them and my vision was partly restored. The room was dark, but the window on the door poured in light sufficient for me to distinguish my surroundings. It didn't take me long to compute my state. I was a prisoner that was for sure. *Whose prisoner?* From all the things I had heard and had been through for the past few trying days, I had no idea.

I was lying on a bed that smelt of cooking oil. I wasn't sure if it was my headache making me smell funny smells or whether it was for real, but one thing that smelt real was blood. I wiped my nose searching for any, but found none. I panicked.

Was I bleeding internally in my nostrils? I sneezed trying to produce some mucus from my nose, but failed as my head ached harder. I reclined back on the small bed and let the ache subside.

It did so after a few minutes. The room had nothing, but the bed, I discovered. I didn't trust myself to stand on my feet to do a little more exploring, so I just sat trying not to think and recover.

The quietness of the room made it complex to differentiate real or imaginary sounds. My jaw ached as I tried to listen harder, filtering the sound as best as I could.

The first thing I heard clearly from the mumbled hisses and vibrations was the opening and closing of a door. Suddenly, the door to the room I was in burst open and I looked away blinded by the light that seared through it. The door was closed back and, with it, high ceiling fixed fluorescent lights flickered on.

I made out a man of not more than sixty wearing a heavy brown coat. Having dealt with a few when I was still in business, I recognised that he was a German with tried and tested eyes. He had dreamy white and black hair and a mouth that seemed like it hadn't opened in months.

As I was sitting on the bed with my eyelids closed, he assumed that I was still groggy and unable to open my eyes. I was known as blind, so to him it must have not mattered.

'Jewel Dean Parkinson,' he announced and threw a book at me. I let it hit me on the chest. He started to laugh.

'Stop acting, Mr Parkinson. I very well know you can see with your eyelids closed,' he waved his hands in front of me.

For a moment, I didn't know what to say or think. I was sure I had never seen this man in my life before. I gazed at the book he had thrown at me. It was a black book with the image of a white mouse. The mouse's eyes had been digitally manipulated to appear as red orbs. The book's title was a simple letter *U*.

'They say third world countries are the best lab holes in the world,' the man continued. 'I could never agree less. Don't you agree, Mr Parkinson?'

'Who are you?' I said shaken from the confusion and how it worsened my headache.

'Call me Dr U,' he said. 'You seriously don't remember me or is it just one of your tricks?'

I was truly lost. 'One of my tricks? Are you insane, what the hell is going on?' I asked more forcefully.

Dr U grinned. 'I want you to give me the encryption keys you developed for Dr V.'

'I don't know what you are talking about. Who is Dr V, what encryption keys?' For a moment, I thought I had gone nuts.

'Don't waste our time, Mr Parkinson. You perfectly know what I am talking about. You thought you could trust V, but let me let you on a little secret. V hates mistakes and you can only count yourself extremely lucky to have lived for so long.'

This more nonsense was getting more annoying by the second. *Was I supposed to know what this man was talking about?*

'I'll make it easier for you, Mr Parkinson, I will be fair. I'll give you exactly an hour to remember the encryption keys otherwise I'm going to be pissed enough to make things personal.'

The man left me confounded. The lights were left on. I spent the next twenty minutes trying hard to remember anything, but all I could remember was being shot at in the burning building after I had foolishly panicked. *Just how long was it from then to now?* I mused.

I felt the book on my lap and opened it. The book made no sense to me. It was written in some sort of code. I searched for any clues on how to read the book and failed.

I gave it up when my head started to pound. I rested on the bed wishing I were dead. The opening of the door made all my senses jump. I sat upright, woozy. The headache returned with full force, but mitigated slowly after a few seconds.

The same man came in, this time carrying a wooden chair and a big brown envelope. He stamped the chair down and sat a few feet from me.

'I believe that was enough time for a man of your intelligence to come up with what I asked for,' Dr U said. 'Are you ready to give me the encryption keys, Mr Parkinson?'

I knew telling him that I had no bloody idea of what he was on about was useless. 'How did I get here?' I tried to get some answers at least.

'Your arm, Mr Parkinson, does it hurt? I believe you were shot,' Dr U said with a murky voice.

I felt for the wound and was surprised that it didn't hurt that much. I unsheathed my top and saw that the wound was cleaned and bandaged. I didn't understand how, to the point where it hadn't registered until now that I had been truly shot.

'Science is a very godlike area of study, Mr Parkinson. The medicine we used to heal your wounds isn't found on the legal and commercial market and yet you are here to prove that it works like a charm,' Dr U laughed in the process. 'I have to ask you though. Being shot at means enemies and in your case where you are wanted for a million-dollar reward, someone shooting you wouldn't want to kill you especially where there is a fire around to destroy positive identification, but whoever did wanted you dead. Who shot you?'

I controlled my breathing, but it didn't do me any good.

'I know nothing. I know absolutely nothing!' I shouted.

'You want me to play games with you, Mr Parkinson? Okay then, let's play,' Dr U said threateningly. He opened the envelope and produced A4 sized photos. He handed them over.

I took them uncertain of what I was going to see. The images thoroughly shocked me. They were pictures of the Tariros lying on my office's desk.

'Those were Dr V's good friends and part of his funding group.

You killed them. Why?' Dr U asked.

It was really ironic and frustrating that the more this man talked to me, the more I got confused. 'I wish I knew what you are talking about, I do.' I said.

'Don't you know these people?'

'I knew them,' I admitted. I knew that lying wasn't going to get me anywhere.

Dr U produced more photos. 'And these,' he handed them to me.

They were photos of Ruth. They caught me unawares. The pictures were taken by a professional surveillance photographer. They were pictures of her leaving her office, house and meeting some old man. The photos were date stamped, but time now meant nothing to me.

I nodded in acknowledgment that I knew her.

This motivated the man as he produced two more photos. These photos really did a number on me. The first was Barbara's photo coming from a black tinted Mercedes and the other was Mike taking a walk with his wife. I swallowed hard. *What the hell was going on?*

'I believe you know that man and of course,' Dr U said pointing at Barbara's photo, 'that breathtakingly attractive woman.'

I swallowed again. My throat seemed dry. 'The fire, I... I... ' I chocked.

'Don't worry, Mr Parkinson, no one was seriously injured by the fire, but then if you wish to know who shot you, I believe you know this woman,' Dr U produced the last photo. He gave it to me.

It was very strange looking at the woman in the photo and not feel like I wasn't looking at a photo of a trained model. The woman looked to be in her late thirties and like she had never had her long hair cut before. I was torn between classifying her as of mixed race or African-American for her nose didn't look like a typical Zimbabwean nose.

In the picture, she wore a black jacket and blue jeans that shaped her long legs and athletic broad waist. The picture must have been taken in winter because the people in her background were all wearing warm clothing.

With her hands in the jacket's pockets, she looked as tall as a model would and I was sure that this woman was hard to forget.

She had a sexual appearance vibrating from her and yet she had an air of almost mysterious innocence. I felt strangely attached to her, and yet something about her eyes and posture made me think she was an Agent from Division. I had come across two or three female Agents from Division over the years and as rumoured, it was difficult to come across a female Agent from Division who wasn't remotely attractive one way or the other.

'I believe this is the person who shot you, Mr Parkinson,' Dr U said.

My vision refocused on the woman on the photo. She didn't look the type of holding a gun and firing it. *If she was possibly Division, were they authorised to shot me on sight, rather than arrest me?* 'Who is she? Why would she shoot me?'

Dr U showed his surprised. He peered at me closely as if not believing me. My gaze remained on the photo as if I was some psychic meditating on the photo of a missing person.

'That is your biological mother, Mr Parkinson. Surely you don't mean to tell me you don't recognise her,' Dr U finally said.

Everything else could have made sense, even the things that had a lower percentage of, but this didn't at all. I had never set my eyes on my biological mother. *If this was indeed my mother, wasn't she supposed to be at least forty-seven plus years old?* There was no way this woman in the picture was my biological mother, it was physically and sensibly impossible.

CHAPTER FOURTEEN

The only thing I was given as the time passed was a glass of sweet water. It tasted as if it had been mixed with sugar cubes. I wasn't given any more answers from that hour.

Dr U had told me that I had been shot by my supposed biological mother. I didn't think straight. I tried, but many questions filled my head that it was extremely difficult to come up with answers that didn't contradict each other.

Why would my mother want to kill me? What had she been doing in the fire? Did my uncle know about all this? Who were these Dr U and Dr V people and what did they mean to me? How was Barbara coping with my sudden disappearance? What the fuck was even going on?

The questions were endless and Dr U's persistence for me to tell him things I didn't know only made it worse. He reappeared constantly and each time I told him I didn't know anything. He even threatened to use unprincipled interrogation techniques on me, but I told him nothing, but the truth. I knew nothing, and if I did, I remembered nothing.

The coded book was my company in solitary. I couldn't think well because I was very hungry. These people were starving me to a psychotic breakdown and it was just a matter of time before I snapped.

I was studying the code in the book when Dr U suddenly budged in as always. He had another man with him. He looked local. The man put a black bag over my head and ordered me to stand up. I hadn't walked in God knew when, so my feet took some time to get accustomed to my lethargic weight. Time passed slowly as we walked. I was inserted into a car and it must have been an SUV judging from its level.

The drive took about twenty minutes and I was transported to a place that had long stony stairs. I tried to make sense of the noise I had heard during the journey. It was mostly traffic noise, nothing helpful to make me decode where I had been or was now.

As I climbed the stairs, I was warned to watch my footing on each step. For someone who had operated blind from a tender age, it was no problem.

The veil was finally taken off and I saw a huge room with a white board, a chair and a metal desk. Apart from that, it was practically empty. Dr U stood close to the table with his arms folded. The man who had brought me left us alone.

'Please sit, Mr Parkinson,' he said gesturing at the chair. I obeyed.

The lights suddenly blacked out. A projector automatically lit up to produce images on the white board. The first image it showed was that of the supposed biological mother.

'Belinda Itai Tapera, age forty-six, born off Irene Bussan and Kevin Tapera. She was part of a secret organisation called *White Haven* belonging to an influential international environmental activist organisation called *Ozone Clouds Corporation*. White Haven is an off-the-budget part of OCC composed of highly skilled intelligence and martially trained environmental partisans – Specialised Agents. They are trained to take care of things when there is an environmental breach that cannot be solved legally or in a satisfying manner. OCC recruited Belinda shortly before she had you,' Dr U explained as a dozen pictures of Belinda appeared on the white board. They were pictures of her from different parts of the world. 'So far, that's what we know about her. Ozone Clouds Corp is mainly based in Switzerland, but it has proxies all over the world, especially in third world countries. They feel like it's their duty to maintain the less polluted developing countries from the far urbanised developed countries,' Dr U continued and many pictures of Ozone Clouds Corp and its proxies appeared. 'This is what most of the world knows.'

I looked on, at the most, glad that I was at least getting some answers to many of my questions.

'In October 1983, OCC covertly formed a scientific division that dealt with issues concerning the preservation of the Ozone layer, endangered species – amongst a few things. It was a group of scientists, many recruited from the countries OCC had proxies and some lured from big organisations like the WHO. I was one of those few. Both of us working in Zambia and Zimbabwe at the time, my best friend at the time, Dr V, was the one who got us in with regards to our advanced work on ultraviolet uses in the developing world.'

I listened intently that the brief seconds he paused seemed like minutes to me. Although I couldn't see him in the dark, I could sense his tenseness.

'We were funded to do our research and projects mainly in and around Lusaka and Harare, compelled to test our experiments at our proxies mostly where laws against science weren't that much detectable or enforced,' Dr U continued. 'During those years, White Haven was mainly devised to take care of lab mistakes at the proxies all over the world, each proxy country having locals recruited to be part of White Haven. Not long after you were born, something happened that caused Dr V and me to leave OCC. The administration of the company thought it was best to deal with us by contracting White Haven Agents in Zimbabwe and Zambia – and worldwide – to make us disappear. We have been living in the shadows since those days and the only way we can ever be safe is if we tie up loose ends and show OCC's management that we are no threat to them anymore. I hope you are getting all of this, Mr Parkinson.'

I was getting all of it except one or more things in the space. 'I want to know why I am to know all this, what am I in all this?' I asked.

'Right now, Mr Parkinson, you are the meaning of all this. You are one of those loose ends OCC doesn't know about. Many people have died because of you. Mr and Mrs Tariro aren't the first people to come out unfortunate in this mess, the list is astonishing.'

I wondered if I had somehow died and was in a pre-hell. It was hard enough suffering for something you knew about. This was worse, like being hanged for a crime you didn't commit.

'Why would anyone pay a million dollars for the apprehension of a blind criminal? Think about it, Mr Parkinson, this is Zimbabwe we are talking about. A million dollars isn't pocket change,' Dr U pointed out.

Of all the things this man had said to me since we first met, this was the most logical. I hadn't had the time to ponder on it, but all of a sudden, it presented itself in front of me.

'Why would anyone want me so bad?'

Dr U snorted in the dark. 'Mr and Mrs Tariro were part of a very strong section of Dr V's secret projects in Zimbabwe. They must be a very big part of the puzzle.'

'But I didn't kill the Tariros,' I protested.

'You seem like you don't even remember your name, Mr Park,' Dr U said. 'How then do you know so confidently that you didn't kill them?'

I didn't know how to respond.

Was I capable of killing? Having no recollection of where I had been made me doubt myself.

'A few months ago, Dr V contacted you and made you an offer. I don't know what that offer was, but one thing I know is that you went through with it. Dr V and I have been working at opposite poles for more than two decades now and he now has a strong part of former White Haven Zimbabwe Agents working for him, making him the influential man he is today.' Dr U paused for a while and pictures began flashing on the white board. I watched stunned. 'These are images of you from a young age. You have been under both our surveillance for a long time, Mr Park.'

'You must be kidding me,' I said aloud. 'What the hell is this?'

'Dr V managed to convince you to work for him to create an essential formula of the encryption to secure data for some kind of biomedical project. Somehow, you developed the encryption keys to his security database using the security resources you developed for your bank months ago. You disappeared with the encryption codes and returned a fortnight ago accused of killing the Tariros,' Dr U gave me some valuable information. 'Everyone interested in this matter is vigorously searching for you right now, some wanting you dead and a few alive.'

I sighed loudly. This was news to me, but it at least gave me some idea of what I was involved in. If only I could remember anything about the time, I was missing. I now knew that Dr U wanted me alive because he wanted the encryption keys. There was no telling what he would do to me once he got them.

I thought of those who wanted me caught or dead. There was my supposed biological mother, the supposed Tariro brothers and the many out there who wanted a million dollars.

'How did you know I could see with my eyelids closed?' I finally asked. Deep down, I knew the answer, but I kept it down there.

Suddenly, there were gunshots outside the room on the other side of the door. I heard the door burst open and a number of shots being fired, and then there was silence.

I had dived to the floor for cover. As I lay down, I felt something trickle toward my left palm. It was liquid and from the odd smell, I figured out that it was possibly Dr U's blood. The only sound in the air was gunshot echoes and the judicious steps of someone. I lay as still as I could.

Lights came on with a flash. I was blinded for a while, but regained my sight to see Dr U lying face siding the floor staring at where I was. His eyes were open and on his head was the mark of a perfectly executed shot. He had died in seconds. I shivered, feeling the person who had shot him walking slowly to where I was.

'Don't move and keep your head down,' the person shouted.

In a normal case, I would have obeyed the command, but the instinct was so strong that I turned my head to see who it was.

The woman was wearing black with an automatic 9mm pistol in her grasp trained at where I was. With my eyelids closed firmly, I looked at her. I was taken aback by how young she looked. Even I in my current state looked older.

'I said don't –' then she stopped to stare at me. We stared at each other long and hard. 'Get up – slowly,' she ordered.

I didn't like the serious tone in her voice so I followed her orders.

She went over and searched Dr U's corpse thoroughly her gun expertly trained at me. The more I saw the woman, the more I was convinced that I was in the middle of a war of more than two sides. This woman couldn't be my biological mother. She looked too young and too attractive to be. I remembered my uncle saying that my bio-mother had been a good-looking prostitute and this woman looked nothing close to the prostitute part. Nothing about this woman made sense at all to me.

I figured having been played by Dr U and tried not to make a silly move. I didn't want to be shot by this woman again. The first time she had shot me – as presumed by Dr U – she must have intended to kill me. I wondered why she hadn't killed me now.

The woman must have found what she was looking for, for she rose and stashed what looked like a colourless credit card into her pocket.

'Belinda?' I said, impulses getting the better of me. My heart seemed to stop as the woman jerked and stared fiercely at me.

'What did you say?' she said firmly.

'I, er – I…' I mumbled, cautiously moving back in small steps.

She advanced towards me and I nearly toppled over. As I had my eyelids closed and could very much make her out, I knew that seeing with eyelids closed wasn't a new thing to her. She must have been one of Dr V's operatives, I assumed. She gazed at the dead Dr U and back at me then at the projector's white board. She frowned and pointed the gun directly at the middle of my forehead.

'Turn around, slowly,' she ordered. I obeyed.

Seconds later, I felt a sharp blow below my head's base and all was black.

CHAPTER FIFTEEN

The irritating aroma penetrated my nose and I vomited and woke up. For someone who hadn't ingested solid food in the past I didn't know days or hours, what I produced were mainly liquids mixed with gastric juices.

My vision was blurred as I fought the indigestion pain down. I moaned and in my effort suddenly realised that I was lying on a carpeted floor. The dust in the carpet was rarely detectable, which told me that place was vacuumed frequently. I didn't have the strength to get up, so I lay there hoping the stomach pains would go away.

I opened and closed my eyes. I saw nothing. I remembered the woman called Belinda knocking me unconscious and wondered if she had damaged my spine in the process. I lay with my eyelids closed hoping that I was in a dark place and needed to get accustomed to the darkness. It didn't work. In a few minutes, I dozed off.

The unlocking of what must have been the door to the room I was woke me up with a start. I was so weak that I couldn't move any muscle. *Was I abducted for the second time? Was it the assumed Dr V now?*

I heard the door open, something of a switch clicked, and then a scream. It shook me all over and sent impulses that made me regain some of my muscle function. I pated around me blind and discovered that nothing was around me. I tried to rise up, but failed.

'Dean?'

I fell back to the floor. *How was this possible?* It made no sense at all. Like my life, nothing ever made sense now.

'Barbara?' I asked unsure.

Was I lost in a wilderness of hallucinations? I felt her weight full on me and discovered that she was hugging me on the floor. I tasted salty moisture on my lips and guessed that it was her tears. What made it extremely odd was that I couldn't see a thing.

'Oh, Dean, oh – Dean,' she said and kissed me full on the lips.

I was too stunned to respond, but didn't stop her. Her hair tickled my face and her soft face skin on mine felt so right I almost felt at peace.

Barbara lay with her head on my chest for a while, sobbing silently. I brushed her hair with my right hand feeling how soft and long it was.

Minutes passed and she finally got off me.

'What's the matter, can't you see me?' she suddenly said.

All I could see was darkness.

'I don't know what happened, but I can't see,' I said.

I raised my hand and she helped me up.

'I don't believe it's you, Dean. You died a month ago.'

'What!' I was shocked that I nearly tumbled on something of object.

'Watch your step,' she warned me and guided me to a sofa.

I sat and waited for her to say something. She did take her time and I knew that whatever I was going to hear wasn't going to be the least normal.

'About a month ago, you and your accomplice tried to outrun two Division Agents at some lodge and you ran into oncoming traffic. You made it to the hospital, but died a day later from brain haemorrhaging. Your accomplice was sent to some maximum prison in South Africa and is awaiting trial for some terrorist charges there, whilst the women who gave the location you were hiding at shared the million-dollar reward,' Barbara said, her tone even. 'You had a private funeral, only attended by your lawyers and Mrs Maguma.'

'Where did you hear this?' I asked.

'The news, the newspapers, almost every media facility in the country had it as major news. Your bank was closed until further notice and clients were compensated. I don't think Silver Bonds will ever be operational again. My employer has been offered to buy it from your lawyers. Since there was no will or any close relative, it was automatically put in your lawyers' trust,' she explained more.

I had yet again lost another month of my memory or time. I didn't know if that was bad or good news. In the end, I made it to be in-between. This was no small thing. The people who had wanted me caught had suddenly conspired me as dead. Nobody was going to look for me now. This led to many questions and answers. If I was now dead, the people wanted me alive and since Belinda hadn't killed me, I was still needed for something. The words *"encryption keys"* came to mind.

How had I ended up at Barbie-J's place? Was she in on the plan, was she a good performer enough to convince me that she hadn't known where I had been? I didn't know whom to trust.

'Your apartment, it was burnt wasn't it?' I said rather silently.

There was silence for a while. 'That part of the building was meant to blow up. I got out, barely, but –' a sob, '– but Fluffy didn't make it.'

'How do you know all this?' I asked curiously, sorry about Fluffy.

There was another brief moment of silence.

'I don't like the tone of your voice, Dean,' she said firmly.

'What?'

'You sound like you don't trust me now, what happened to you?' she said in an offended tone.

'I just don't trust anyone at the moment,' I said truthfully. I needed facts. So far, I had none.

'That really hurts me, Dean,' Barbara said. 'You want to know how I knew that someone tried to blow up the building and make it look like an electrical fault. Your uncle was kind enough to tell me.'

'My what?' I nearly stood up.

'What do you remember now? Have you forgotten everything from before you died – disappeared again?' Barbara asked. 'He is the one who brought me to this safe house where nobody can find me without first going through tedious security,' she poured it all out on me.

I opened my eyelids and what happened is that I *saw* everything. It was like a miracle. I didn't believe it at first so I closed my eyelids and opened them several times.

'What is it, Dean? Don't tell me you are having a seizure,' Barbara said standing up. She came over.

I blinked again and for sure I could now see with my eyelids open. *What in the world had happened to me?* I tried to think. Somewhere deep in my soul, there was undefined joy. I could *see* normally, I could *see*. I smiled as I looked at where BJ was. Her beauty seemed enhanced and I could see that she had grown some fat making her hips wider and bosom bigger. I suddenly remembered that she was pregnant.

BJ looked hard at me and gaped. 'How is it possible?' she said.

I looked away and closed my eyes pretending that everything was the way it was.

'Don't you dare, Dean,' she said and came over and turned my head to her with both palms at the sides. 'Open your eyes, now!' she screamed.

I opened my eyes and she looked as if she had zoomed in.

'You can see me? I know you can see me. What did they do to you?' she said staring me directly in the eyes.

It was incredible how this lady could read me. It was no use lying to her whoever she was. Her attractiveness was just enough to send me reeling in a corner of emotion.

'I don't know, BJ, I just don't know anything,' I said. I told her about what I could remember. She listened without interjecting.

I came to the part where I was supposed to tell her about Belinda, but I didn't. I figured that she must had triggered the burning down of BJ's flat. A lot of time had passed in-between then and now.

She was touched that I had nearly died risking my life to go into a burning building in an effort to rescue her whilst not knowing if she had been in the building or not.

'I did it for baby Dean,' I teased her.

She grinned at me. 'Yeah, right,' she said and gave me a look so appealing that it was torture to look at her and not have elevated thoughts.

'How did you meet Choirmaster?' I finally asked. I needed and wanted to know.

'The night you left to meet him, I suddenly noticed a blue car outside the flat. It was a surveillance team watching my apartment. I thought it was the police, Agents or something. Then the building suddenly shook as the electricity station exploded. Within minutes, two men came, knocked me out with some kind of chemical, and took me away. The next thing I remember was Mike and me in this big house being told that we were in danger and were going to be put under house protection at certain safe houses,' Barbara breathed, stopping for a few seconds.

'He told us who he was and was very pissed when you suddenly went missing again. He said he had people watching me and Mike as protection and that he had been foolish enough not to put someone on you the day you were shot and taken by Dr U. Mike was pretty upset when he was told that he wasn't going back to work until all this was solved. I too had to leave work.'

I listened and wondered. I didn't say anything.

'Mike and his family are at another safe house close to your uncle. Your uncle said it's good that way because of the child and wife. The safe houses are too big though. Your uncle must be a very rich influential man.'

'You have no idea – he is after all the Choirmaster,' I said and looked around the room. The window blinds were closed. 'Does my uncle know I'm here?'

'God, no, nobody knows where you are. I told you that they declared you dead, but I guess that didn't fool him. He must have known, but never told me. I have to call him on a secure line, shall I?'

I had no choice. I nodded. 'Do you have a computer around this place?' I asked.

BJ stared at me and laughed. 'Are you serious?' she said.

'This place is like a small island of resources – a computer is like nothing here. Come and I'll show you the library. You can choose which computer you want to use then.'

After calling my uncle, BJ took me on a tour of the house. She didn't know where it was, but I had a feeling that it was in a rocky suburb. The house was a vast beauty that had many trees surrounding it as if to hide it from the rest. The grounds were spread long and the lawns made it difficult to cross them to the main house without being seen. I made out a few cameras fixed here and there together with night heat sensors.

As we walked around, we came across three men who nodded at us. They were dressed as gardeners, but I knew that they were more than that. I felt so much respect for the Choirmaster.

BJ held my hand and snuggled in closer as we walked. I could feel her happiness vibrate and sensed her smiles. I was stunned that someone could feel like this so much and being next to me at the same time.

The library was a masterpiece. Four computer sets were fixed at various angles of the room on and ready to use. I chose the one that didn't look too high tech. I logged onto the web and searched for info on *Ozone Clouds Corp*. It did exist and from the way it hit the search engine, it was indeed a huge company. It had centres all around the world and was famous for its environmental awareness and its stern implementation of environmental laws.

I goggled for *White Haven* and saw that it was masked to be a financial entity of OCC. There was no mention of it recruiting and training hired guns or contract workers to work on OCC's covert research facilities.

Everything Dr U had told me about OCC was genuine. I figured if it was all true. *What about Belinda?* I felt for my jacket's pocket and found Dr U's book together with the photo he had given me to keep. *After a month, how was it possible that I had this in my possession, unless planted?* I stared at the photo for a long time. Yes, the same woman had shot Dr U.

'What is that?' BJ suddenly sneaked up behind me.

I jerked and the book cluttered onto the keyboard.

BJ snatched the photo away from me and stared at it. I witnessed as her eyes darkened. 'Who is this?'

Her tone was undoubtedly filled with strains of jealousy. I resisted the urge to grin. It was lovely to feel so wanted. 'I don't think you need to worry about it,' I snatched the photo back and placed it in my pocket.

'So you met someone else during your disappearance? Why didn't you tell me?' she wasn't pleased at all.

'I told you everything. Please be reasonable, it's not like it really matters,' I tested the waters.

'Don't mock me, Dean,' she said. 'I lost my virginity to you, damnit! I'm carrying your child – it matters a lot.'

Hearing it spoken made it all official. My heart floated excitedly. 'I believe I lost my virginity to you too – if you must know,' I said looking back at the computer. 'I just wanted to know if it mattered.'

'You could have just asked,' she shrugged. 'Who is she?'

Her persistency nagged me. Telling her seemed like a very bad idea. 'It's better if you don't know, for now,' I assured her.

She wasn't pleased, but she said nothing. So many things had happened in such a short and long time and not knowing some things was far better off.

I goggled myself and BJ's story was confirmed. I was said to have died an infamous criminal. My estate was to be sold and it hurt me that Ms Parkinson's old home was going to be seen as the reminiscence of a blind mad man who had killed his neighbours. When I thought of how I could see normally now, I felt as if I was a newborn with a new future. How it had happened didn't matter that much to me than how I had ended up at BJ's safe house. *Had it been my uncle?* From BJ's reactions, my uncle hadn't known. He had promised to come over as soon as possible. He took his time much to my surprise.

The Choirmaster arrived around eleven P.M. His first reaction was to hug me and, as someone who had thought I could already see normally, he wasn't surprised when I looked at him without my dark glasses.

'Dean, my boy, I knew they were fabricating it – I knew it,' he said hugging me once more.

I was touched to see him emotional. Everybody knew that he wasn't an emotional person. I was stunned to see that when he looked at BJ, there were glimpses of an odd shyness from him. I guessed BJ's features made him anxious.

I told him everything I knew and he was indeed surprised. For someone who was used to knowing everything before it happened, it was a start. He promised to find out more details and excused himself by claiming that I needed more time with my *wife*. BJ beamed at this statement and the Choirmaster laughed at my uneasiness.

'Mrs DJ Parkinson – that sounds nice,' BJ crooned loud enough for me to hear.

I was going to have a baby with this woman and yet I had no recollection of sleeping with her or ever seeing her naked. It was ironic, very disturbing. As she slept beside me that night in her cosy bed, I studied the *U-book* searching for clues. *How was it possible for a blind banker to create encryption keys for some project? Wasn't that stuff meant for people like Mike?*

I slept sound that night. I woke up early to find BJ missing from the bed. My hyper ears picked up her voice and I could hear her whispering to someone else. Seconds later, I figured that she was on the phone.

'… He is asleep now. I don't think he knows yet,' she was saying.

I was now fully awake my heart pounding.

'… It's only a matter of time – it's just a matter of hours or days, we have to be patient,' she continued. 'I'll keep in touch.'

I pretended to be asleep when she walked back in. I was afraid my heart was going to sell me out for I could hear it beat loudly. BJ walked over to her side of the bed and snuggled in.

'Are you awake, Dean?' she startled me.

Her ability of reading me scared the hell out of me. *Did she know that I had overheard her?* Ignoring her could have made her suspicious so I mumbled something as if half awake.

She returned to sleep and I had my mind racing. What I had been afraid of was nearly coming true. *Who had BJ been talking to?* If I asked her, I would make her awareness sharper. I needed to find out on my own.

Not less than an hour later, I woke up and found BJ sitting in her bed her mind seemingly far away. She was staring straight ahead into the distance and probably for the first time I saw worry. She was troubled by something new and I wondered if it was the phone call. I forced my curiosity down and refrained from asking her about it.

'A coin for your thoughts,' I said and was suddenly hit by the realization that as an official dead man, I didn't even have a coin in my pocket. I no longer had my wallet and the credentials in it. All I had was Dr U's book and Belinda's photo, not forgetting my normal eyesight mysteriously attained.

'Morning to you too, Dean,' she said soberly.

'You sound troubled, are you okay?' I asked curiously than concerned.

She smiled briefly. 'I'm trying hard to convince myself that I'm not immersed in a fast phased dream, but it seems impossible.'

It was as if she had been reading my mind during the night. I put my hands behind my head. My fingers ran over something new and I felt it again. *Was it a horizontal scar?* The more I felt it, the more my mind raced. *How in the world could I have a scar on the back of my head and not known about it?*

I bent myself arching forward. 'Do I have a scar here?' I had to be sure.

BJ's hands ran over my head and she shrugged. 'Yes, why do you ask? Don't you know about it?'

'If I did, would I be asking?' My mood got the better of me. I heated up slowly, trying hard to stay calm.

'That looks old. Surely it must be years since you had it,' BJ was heated up by my retort.

Years? I thought.

I was sure I hadn't had that scar when I woke up with a blank mind that day in my office. I hadn't had the scar during my stay at BJ's apartment. *Was it loss of memory or something else had happened to me the time I had blacked out during the burning flat?* It was now impossible to tell what I could and couldn't remember about my life lately.

'The sooner I get my memory back, I think the better,' I said lying back into the bed.

'Regarding how extremely interesting my life has been since I met you, Dean, I couldn't agree more,' BJ concurred openly.

I thought of my old life. There was no possible way of reclaiming it. Everything I had had was no longer mine. My money, my qualifications – all was gone. I was now a ghost, a man with no identity. The only things before this life I had was BJ and the Choirmaster. The main key to start afresh was to go over the old things and, unfortunately, I only had a forty percent idea of what they were. I knew that by unlocking some cubes of my brain, I was going to discover certain things, things that were going to make me understand why certain things were happening to me and things that I would wish I hadn't tried to uncover. I was no longer Dean J Parkinson, so I couldn't die twice.

Chapter Sixteen

The Choirmaster returned at the same time that night. He brought quite a lot of info with him. Together with it was a compiled dossier of the Tariros. I remembered losing the briefcase he had given me the night I had been abducted by Dr U. He hadn't asked what had happened to it, so I had wisely said nothing about it. After a long boring day watching TV with BJ at the safe house, this was a pick of pace.

'I did some digging and what you told me yesterday pans out with what I found,' Choirmaster said as we sat in the library, BJ closely beside me. I felt a bit uncomfortable with her beside me in the presence of my uncle. I had barely looked her in the eye that day because of my ever-rising suspicions about her since that morning's phone call. 'OCC has a proxy in Zimbabwe, quite a small one, but it's very hard to distinguish. It's disguised as a beverage company. However, White Haven has recruited quite a number of locals, people who start as desperate citizens struggling to make a living. They train them into highly skilled private Agents for on-going and abandoned OCC projects. Dr V and Dr U were tasked to operate their experiments in the Southern Africa region way back in the mid-eighties and when they went rouge, OCC disowned them and abandoned future projects in the region. However, these two remained in Africa knowing very well that White Haven was assigned to terminate them.'

I listened on as he spoke, hoping to hear something new. Most of the stuff he was saying I had heard already from Dr U.

'OCC's proxy was one of Silver Bond's biggest clients and the proxy lured several established local businessmen and women to fund its local projects without aligning any undesired attention to it. As I discovered lately, you were one of those businessmen.'

'Me?' I asked stunned.

'Yes, son, you. Why do you think the Tariros were so fond of you?' Choirmaster enlightened me. This was news to me. 'You were a young blind African raised by an old wealthy white lady and they took you in like their son. Weren't you ever suspicious?'

I had never had suspicions and having them brought to my consciousness didn't appeal to me. It was one thing feeling guilty because I didn't know what had happened to the Tariros. It was another feeling having been played and living lies.

'I think your Dr V was working on something new and you played a part in securing his work. Dr U's people must have found out and stolen whatever it was. They kidnapped you and before they could make any progress with you, Dr V's people reacquired their stuff and somehow you ended up here. Whether you gave them the encryption codes and access data, I don't know as you yourself don't, but assuming that they let you go, you must have.'

If I had, did that mean I was free now? I produced the photo as planned and held it in front of him. 'Do you know this person?' I asked.

He stared at the picture and took it. 'No, who is that?' he asked back, studying the picture.

'The person who killed Dr U,' I said.

Choirmaster knew who my biological mother was and he not knowing who Belinda was confirmed the doubts I had about what Dr U had told me. I hadn't told anyone about Belinda yet. I somehow felt like I needed to present it at the right time.

Many days passed as I tried hard to regain my lost memory. I went over many techniques I had printed from the internet, but none seemed to work. YouTube's self-help videos didn't help either. The only time I felt like I was close to remembering something was when I was going over Dr U's encoded book. It was so frustrating to gaze page after page and feel a few seconds from the truth, but never getting there.

The lines in the book were written using symbols and roman numerals.

Barbara gave it up on her third day. I thought of Mike, but BJ said that I couldn't contact him unless it was strictly necessary, as the Choirmaster had warned. The success of the two Mayas staying undetected depended on them not communicating just in case someone was on the lookout. Choirmaster had cautioned us that Dr V's men weren't to be underestimated.

Then and there, we didn't know if it was safe for BJ and her brother to return to their normal lives. Until he was a hundred percent positive, my uncle was determined to keep them hidden.

The key to decoding Dr U's book was to remember the encryption codes, BJ had assessed. I too had come to the same conclusion. I studied encryption and decryption from the net, but I felt silly when I couldn't make sense of any of it.

'Why don't we give the book to your uncle or let him pass it on to Mike,' BJ suggested after another week of obsession with my little black book. 'They may have better luck than us.'

'This is something I have that might give me my memory back,' I said. 'I believe I need to keep it close.' I finished off the statement by staring hard at her.

Getting the message that I didn't want to argue about it, Barbara raised her eyebrows and shook her head. 'Whatever you say.'

Right before I went to rest that day, I passed by a guest suite and my ears caught sounds coming from it. I stopped subconsciously and listened. It was BJ on the phone and this time she was whispering rapidly. I thought of jumping on her and demanding for some answers, but I couldn't move. I made out words that involved something like encryption codes and routers. It appeared as if she was talking to a superior and an authoritative one for that matter.

I tiptoed away afraid that she was going to catch me eavesdropping.

First the Tariros and now BJ? I was heart stricken to contemplate on it. Deep down, I think I had known it all along. Someone who looked like BJ couldn't sleep or fall in love with a blind banker. My doubts were rewarded now. BJ must be working for Dr V and that explained why I had woken up at this house of all places. *Had my uncle figured it out yet?*

Whose child was BJ carrying for it surely wasn't mine? Was she part of White Haven, devastatingly attractive and a good actor to lure a stupid man such as myself? What awaited me was going to be very difficult. I had to put on a performance and act as if I wasn't on to her. It was going to be hard, but I knew my life depended on it.

The first dream I had about Ms Parkinson was pretty ordinary. She was at my ex-house pointing at it her eyes red and weepy. I knew it was my subconscious feeling guilty about letting her house get sold, to be let go in such a way. There was nothing I could do to reverse that issue and was probably going to live with it for the rest of my life.

I continued working on the book. BJ sensed that I was avoiding her most of the time. I couldn't help it, but I was careful enough to keep an honest face. Her pained expression ate me up. She was a truly gifted actress, I thought.

I couldn't afford to feel bad for her, but I did anyway. Every time I looked at her when she wasn't staring at me, my heart shrank. I wished I had never met her because if I somehow managed to get out of this shit I was in, Barbara was going to be like an untreatable cancer for the rest of my miserable life.

The dreams involving Ms Park recurred and more advanced every night. This time she was pointing at a specific location, which I couldn't make out clearly. It was either a shade I had played in when I was young or a dog's kennel. As I had never had any pets growing up, I figured it was the former.

Days passed slowly with no success with the book. Coincidentally, I kept running into BJ's secretive calls. Her frustrated expressions made me guess that my being unable to remember the codes was beginning to affect her.

One night, when I had spent the day in the library studying more about decrypting data, she undressed right in front of me. I didn't want to, but my head forced me to look. Her belly was swelling nicely along with everything else. I swallowed hard and stared like an idiot.

'What?' she stared back at me. 'It's not like you haven't seen everything before.'

Her tone was meant to mock me and it worked. I looked away and my heart raced wildly. I was afraid she was going to get in bed naked and my fears were caught in mid-air as she did. It was obvious that she had one thing in mind. I shivered badly knowing that no matter how hard I tried, I couldn't resist. Some temptations were just too overpowering and this was arguably the highest-ranking one.

High adrenaline messed me up and the next thing I remembered was shivering uncontrollably and seeing a sharp blue light.

Chapter Seventeen

The blue light brought with it peace. I looked around and saw that I was at the centre of a football stadium in a dark night. I had a battered old torch, wearing a coat that was dripping at the sides with the rain that was being stopped from drenching me by a medium sized umbrella.

I was waiting anxiously and I checked the time. The glass of my watch was covered by cold stream. I wiped it clean and made the clock hands making it half past eight evening time. I suddenly heard noises other than the rain and looked up to see two people walking towards where I was. They both had umbrellas and wore black overcoats. I prod the ground nervously with my walking stick and adjusted my dark glasses.

'Mr Parkinson,' the man in front greeted me.

The other remained a distance back and with the way he was looking around, I knew he was a professional bodyguard. The man in front of me looked old and was Caucasian.

'You are late,' I said.

'I'm sorry, Mr Parkinson, my boss had me taking care of something else,' the man said.

'I've kept my end of this deal. It's now your turn,' I said confidently.

The man produced a cigarette and took his time lighting it. He drew twice and blew in the rain. He looked unnervingly calm.

'Do you need that?' he said pointing at my walking stick. 'Sorry. I had forgotten, only a few of us know you can actually see.'

I frowned and fought my anger from surfacing. 'As I said, as we agreed, I'll finish off and give you your ECs after the surgery.'

'I thought you wanted to meet my boss too?'

'And that too,' I said annoyed.

The man laughed and threw his cigarette into the rain. It fell a distance before the water lit it out. 'What makes you think you haven't met him or her already?'

'I don't have time to play games,' I said furiously. 'I'll give the codes to your boss personally after he gives me what he promised.'

'What is to stop us from getting them if we want to?'

For someone who had come fully prepared, I laughed. It unsettled the man who stared at me as if I had gone nuts. 'I'm the only one who knows how your data is secured and how to retrieve it. I promise you now that if you mess with me in any way, you can go and tell him to kiss his research goodbye.'

The man nodded and ended up laughing as well.

This did counteract and unsettle me. 'Very well, they don't call you the Blind Banker for nothing. I'll pass the word to Dr V. See you at the party tomorrow, Mr Parkinson – good evening.'

I watched them leave and my head seemed to explode at the same.

'Dean, Dean, wake up, Dean – are you okay?'

I opened my eyes and my blurry vision took time to adjust. In a nightgown, Barbara was on top of me, a wet towel in one hand.

'What happened?' I slurred my words.

'You, you – I don't know what happened,' she said, her face filled with fear.

'You have been unconscious for two minutes or so.'

I tried to get up and felt my body covered with mounds of sweat. I knew I had had a sudden flashback. *Should I tell her?* I thought. I decided not to. She would tell her boss and something was bound to happen. I tried to think of a way I could tell the Choirmaster without letting Barbara know.

I didn't sleep that night. Whatever BJ had planned to do had been forgotten or postponed and I was grateful for it.

Two days passed and I didn't have another flashback. It was so frustrating because I had been hoping that that was beginning of my memory recovery process. BJ bugged me every chance she got. I knew that she couldn't wait to get her hands on the *eCodes*. Choirmaster was out of play for unusually long that I began to fear that he had forgotten all about me. I quizzed on whether it was safe to tell him about my flashback. *Had it been a real memory or some kind of vivid hallucination?*

Apart from trying to decipher Dr U's small book, I focused some of my attention on discovering what had caused the flashback. In the end, I discovered that it had been BJ. Her actions that night had aroused many emotions and chemicals in my body to the extent where some switch had been triggered. BJ hadn't made any more moves on me afraid I would seize and have a heart attack. Part of me wished she would. I badly needed my memory back and that seemed like the only possible way I could get it. Searching for an alternative, I used the internet to search for porn. It didn't do me any good for it was apparently immaterial. Live action pretty much was no match. Video and pictures weren't real and I was more frustrated.

'What are you watching? Is that –?' Barbara came into the library. I was very sorry I hadn't heard her coming in. Her eyes widened.

'Is that graphic, Dean?' she was undeniably shocked.

I clicked the window shut and didn't dare look back at her. I heard her walking toward where I was. My heart beat faster with each step she took.

'Men are all the same after all,' she said sitting down.

I turned around and looked at her. She had a scornful look on her face.

'What is that supposed to mean?' I tried not to feel guilty. She had no right to question my actions when she was a matter of fact lying to me all this time.

'Here I am and yet you're looking for porn to turn yourself on. What in the world is going on, Dean?' she snapped at me. 'You've been acting so strange these past few weeks, like I offended you in any way.'

You call pretending to love me and lying about carrying my child innocent? I thought furiously.

'It's the eCodes. I can't seem to be making any progress. I'm sorry,' I said softly. I didn't want to make her cautious. These people were good, so good enough to have one of them so close to me that even the Choirmaster was fooled.

'I've an idea,' BJ suddenly said, my insecurities all forgotten.

'Let's hear it,' I said.

'Do you have any knowledge of how your bank was constructed?'

I looked at her stunned. 'Of course, I was the one who built it!'

'I mean – do you remember?' she justified herself.

It was a good point, so I thought about it. Surprisingly, I remembered quite a lot. 'Yes, I remember,' I said wanting to hear her point of view.

'I think you should give me details like the company which built it. You said Dr U said the technology used to secure the research's data is at Silver Bond. The construction company must know what it is, don't you think so?'

I thought about it. It was a good idea. If I knew what kind of technology, perhaps I would remember the eCodes and how I had developed them. It was a long shot.

'Why you? We can just inform Choirmaster.'

'Just like we informed him about the book, hey?' she challenged. 'Don't tell me that you aren't tired of this place already. I need to do something and seeing this constructor of yours is a first step.'

Staying at a very big house, not getting out and seeing new people was really straining. I spent most of my time on the internet so it affected me less. For BJ, it was complex. Watching TV from the morning until nighttime became a boring habit. She needed some fresh air just as I needed answers.

'What do you suggest?' I asked.

'I suggest you tell me who built your bank and I'll visit them tomorrow morning masquerading as a prospective client,' she said confidently. Her pregnancy was beginning to show off its belly. She was in no condition to move around and not get noticed. *But then, why did I care?*

'I'll come with you,' I said, not looking at her.

'Why?'

It was a question that asked a lot questions. 'I don't know,' I said feeling stupid.

Barbara frowned. 'How caring you must be. I thought something like I was carrying your child would be more like it,' she said wounded.

For someone who had had his eyes opened, knowing we didn't mean anything to each other, I didn't give a shit. 'I meant that as well,' I acted.

She wasn't satisfied. 'You aren't coming with me.'

'Why?' I was prepared to argue.

'Because you are dead,' she said simply.

That brought me back to the ground. It would appear very bizarre if I was suddenly to walk into my prior constructor's offices. By going out into the world, BJ was going to expose herself to Dr V's people. That was what the Choirmaster knew. I knew something else. BJ was part of Dr V's people, so it didn't matter if she was seen around or not.

I thought of warning my uncle the following day when BJ was supposed to do her thing, but decided against it. Dr V was a very powerful person, there was no telling what he would do that the Choirmaster if the Choirmaster suddenly dealt with BJ after my revelations.

That evening, I planned to have a bath before I worked on the book again. I ran into BJ as she was just coming from the bathroom. A shower cap covered her hair and she had a huge white towel wrapped around her freshly washed body. Knowing very well that she didn't have anything, but the towel on, I felt very uneasy. She smiled at me as she passed and left me fighting myself not to look at her as she walked away.

I entered the bathroom and my body suddenly began to sweat profusely. Before I could make sense of anything, my knees buckled and I collapsed to the floor.

The room had blue lights and numbers were projected onto the walls like I was in a matrix. I looked around and saw that I was in a room full of computers. With me was a small book with numerous numbers. After studying for a while, I suddenly realized that these numbers were bank account numbers for my bank.

They ran in a pretty random sequence. More scrutiny made me aware that the way they were strung was in a series of odd numbers, meaning that they stood for something – every one of them. I wasn't so sure what they stood for, but I had a hint that I had been the one who had created these sequences and series.

On the screen of the mainframe computer was a cube made from binary numbers. My face was sweaty and my stomach grumbled. I was very hungry like someone who hadn't eaten anything for days. Suddenly, the door to the room opened and in came the man I had met at the stadium.

'Have you finished?' he asked.

I focused my attention at him, my dark glasses flashing with various lights. 'I'll tell you when I'm finished,' I said angrily.

'Dr V wants you to be quick. The time period of funding is getting near,' he said.

'When I am ready, I'll tell you,' I said with finality.

The man shook his head and left.

I stared at the screen and made a few calculations. Like a curtain being drawn in front in front of me, I finally came out with the perfect solution. I wrote the keys down in sequence and had my heart beat faster with excitement. The result was seven number lines each with seven symbols. Together I had forty-nine symbols that made the final eCodes. I memorised them and had an idea. I called my handler.

'Finally, Mr Parkinson, you did it,' he said excitedly.

I handed him two colourless credit-like cards and printed the *49Symb* or *7x7eCs* on four pieces of paper. He pointed at the screens and I knew that he wanted me to test them. I tested them and they were successful.

'Good, Mr Parkinson, that wasn't so hard, was it?'

'How about you cash in your part of the deal.'

'Of course, of course,' he said. 'I'll get back to you. If only you hadn't tried to be difficult before the party, things could have been smoother. I'll talk to Dr V.'

I was left in the room for a few minutes before two men came and took me away.

The memory faded and I found myself on the bathroom floor sweating. My body looked as if I was just coming from a shower. The flashback made little sense to me, but I figured that after all this fuss, I had given the man the wrong keys. Dr V was looking for the eCodes and I knew that whatever he had stored using my bank's data vault security system was locked away forever if the eCodes were never found. Somehow, I knew that if I had built the system, I would have created a system that would corrupt the data stored beyond repair if any other methods were used to breach its security. Dr V must have known it. I was probably the most important person in the world to Dr V and his people at the moment.

Chapter Eighteen

I watched as BJ dressed as an Executive. Her growing belly showed a little. I knew it was just show for me to believe that she was trying hard to help me even to risk exposure. By now, I was very positive that BJ was one of Dr V's people. Everything pointed to that possibility. I didn't enjoy it the least, but I lived with it.

'Wish me luck,' she said smiling at me.

I weakly smiled back. 'Good luck with the people at Mosaic Architects, I hope you get what you are looking for.'

'Some vote of confidence you got there, Dean,' she grinned.

I inwardly admitted that she looked cool in a black suit – being pregnant or not. I suppressed the emotions within me. Last time I had let them take over, I had had two flashbacks. Although it was good to some extent, the headaches I had afterwards were devastating.

BJ left a few minutes later. I was all alone at the house and ideas flooded my mind. I had to do something. I tried to decode the small book, but with no success. I had thought that my last flashback would at least give me back some parts of my memory. It didn't.

Practically, my brain was still the same.

Bored, I had a walk around the vast grounds of the house. I ended up resting at one of the fixed benches. Suddenly, a cellphone rang behind me. In a flowerpot, near the bench, was the phone. I took it and wondered if one of the men disguised as gardeners had left it there. If so, what was I supposed to do? All I knew was that my uncle had hired these men to protect BJ and BJ was currently MIA. The phone kept on ringing. I was compelled to answer it, as it didn't show any signs of stopping.

'Listen to me very carefully, boy,' the voice behind the call greeted me. 'Do exactly as I say if you want to live.'

'I'm sorry, what?' I said scared.

'Do as I say, Dean, I'm watching you right now,' the voice said firmly.

I was confused. A few seconds later, a *phhht* suddenly came from behind me. It was a silenced shot fired from a rifle – a warning shot?

I looked around to see no one. I was afraid that if I didn't do as asked I would be either shot or worse. I followed the commands given, no matter how silly they appeared.

Fifteen minutes later, I found myself going through a hole in the fence that surrounded the grounds. It was located on a downhill slope that was vegetated by many trees and bushes. There were security cameras and sensors installed at various spots. They all looked lifeless.

Down the slope, I espied a black Mazda 3. I walked toward it. The cars windows were tinted so I couldn't see if anyone was in it or not. I opened the car's door as asked and got in. The doors automatically locked behind me. I looked at the driver and my heart skipped a bit. I tried to open the door in an attempt to escape, but it was useless.

'Be still, Dean,' the driver said and started the engine.

The car left tyre marks as it gunned from the parked position.

'Who are you?' I asked, nearly stammering.

'Don't tell me that you don't know already,' the driver said.

An advanced tablet was set near the automatic gear stick. I looked at it and saw the screen divided in four. Looking closely, I discovered that it showed footage of various randomly rotating camera angles to the safe house. The gardeners were looking for me, now aware of my absence. I knew Choirmaster was going to be pissed. *How was BJ going to explain my sudden disappearance to him?* I thought. *Or had BJ left for good and I was now being taken away as well?* My uncle would never discover what happened.

'You aren't my mother,' I suddenly said.

Belinda laughed and removed her small wireless earphone throwing it at the passenger seat. 'Your father was a funny man too,' she said.

It wasn't what she said, but how she said it that annoyed me.

'You know my father?' I was stunned.

Belinda laughed again. She drove so fast I was afraid her laughing was going to nail us to an oncoming car or truck.

'Your father and I were early college days' lovers – then we had you and everything changed,' her voice was so sweet that I was so consumed by it to forget where I was and what she had done to Dr U and his people.

'How old are you?'

'I know many people say I don't look my age,' Belinda said with a wry smile this time. 'I guess if people saw us together they would consider I was your wife than your mother.'

'You aren't my mother,' I protested. I didn't want her to manipulate me like BJ had.

'Wake up, Dean!' she shouted. Her tone sounded odd for it didn't have any waves of anger. It was filled with hurt.

Five minutes passed as she drove frequently changing her speed. I witnessed us leaving the suburbs into the city then leaving the city again.

'Where are you taking me?' I finally asked, tired of the curiosity.

'You'll see when we get there,' she answered.

'You work for Dr V, don't you?' I asked knowing that after this, it was going to be very hard to get any answers from her.

'I work for no one,' she said firmly.

We reached a road that led to a hill. It was almost paved like the ones in Chisipite. We drove for ten minutes before we reached the house. It was huge, almost like the safe house, but looked as if it hadn't been used for years. Weeds grew all over and the outer paint of the house was fading its original colour.

'Come with me,' Belinda ordered as she got out of the car. 'Someone is eagerly waiting for you.'

I had no choice, but to obey. I wondered if Dr V was that eager to see me. *Did he think I could remember the eCodes?*

Belinda produced a big key and unlocked the enormous front door. She pushed it open and stale air greeted us. The inside was dark with meagre light fizzing through some of the high windows of the foyer. Two long staircases led to two different wings of the house. Belinda locked the door and made me follow her up the right staircase.

We passed five doors in a corridor that was barely lit by two light bulbs. Upon reaching the sixth door, Belinda stopped and listened. She knocked once then twice after a brief pause. I heard noises come from the inside. The door opened after a minute. I entered and was almost knocked off my feet with shock.

'Barbara?' I said.

Belinda and Barbara in the same picture confirmed my hunches about being played by Barbara.

'It didn't take you that long,' BJ said to Belinda.

Belinda walked over to a huge table at the far end of the room. On it was a closed laptop. She placed her tablet on top of it and sat with a heavy sigh.

'He didn't make it challenging enough,' she smiled.

'So after all this time, you have been playing me?' I started, my voice saturated with anger. 'You've been working for him all this time, how stupid of me!'

Barbara stared at me. 'Working for who, what are you talking about, Dean?'

'Oh, quit it, Barbara, did you really think I wasn't going to find out?' I shouted. *Was her real name even Barbara?* I thought.

'Sit down, Dean,' Belinda said firmly.

'Don't dare tell me what to do you whore,' I was now frenzied beyond control.

'Don't call your mother a whore, Dean!' Barbara shouted back.

I was about to shout back when the words registered into my mind. 'Where is your boss, Barbara? I want to see him now!'

Barbara looked more stunned. 'What are you talking about? What boss?'

'Come on, Barbara, Dr V, of course,' I said laughing sarcastically. 'The one you have been calling for the past few days updating him on me.'

'Are you insane?' she screamed at me. The look on her face made me feel a bit odd. 'I don't know Dr V. You are the one who knows him.'

'You are lying!' I said.

She frowned. 'Okay, okay I know who Dr V is, but why call him my boss?'

I sneezed and felt my skin burn. *I was right after all,* I thought.

'You are a very good actress, Barbara, or is that even your real name? You really had me going on for a while. I can't blame myself though. Dr V really chose you well – your beauty, style and all got me. And the pregnancy, now that was a masterpiece. Pretending to be pregnant with my child just at the right moment and pretending to love me even if I was blind. Wow!' I clapped my hands in applause of mockery.

Barbara stared at me as if she wanted to kill me. Her next reaction baffled me greatly. She burst into tears and went to sit on a sofa crying. For someone who had expected a much more opposite reaction from her, I blinked hard confused.

Belinda stood up and walked up to me. She looked very angry. Before I could rethink of what to do in the process, I was slapped hard on the face.

'That is for my grandchild,' she shouted. 'Now sit your idiotic ass down before I force you to.'

The slap made me sit without complaint. I knew what this woman was capable of. I didn't want to test her patience.

'I was the one calling Barbara for the past few days,' Belinda said after sitting down herself. 'I'm the one who brought her here.'

'Why?' I asked.

'To keep her safe and to keep her baby, my grandchild, safe,' Belinda said with such confidence I wondered if I had had it all wrong.

'What are you saying?' I was really confused. 'To keep safe from whom when you are the one who works for the people who are after me? Shooting me, killing people like it's some sort of game.'

'You don't know the half of it, Dean, so listen very carefully,' Belinda said. The room looked coolly furnished and I wondered how long it had been used. 'I used to work for Dr V because that was the only way I was going to convince him to keep you alive. I was forced to do some pretty nasty things. One of them was killing Dr U.'

'I don't understand, where does Barbara come in all this and why did you put me at the safe house?' I asked looking at Barbara who had stopped crying, but looked very sad.

'Barbara isn't what you think she is. She is an innocent person caught up in a big mess. You're extremely lucky to have someone like her in your life, Dean,' Belinda said softly. I saw signs of sadness from her eyes. 'I put you at the safe house under Dr V's direct orders. They first gave you the surgery and, knowing how successful it was, they figured that the only way they could reverse the mind programming process and possibly get your memory back to give them the real eCodes was to have you close to something that really mattered, Barbara.'

Few things now made sense, if this woman was telling the truth.

'How do I lose a month of my life just like that, and not

remember anything from the point where you shot Dr U and knocked me unconscious?' I was confused.

'The surgery you had took not less than twenty-four hours, give or take. After effects were said to be some memory loss and they kept you under for more than a week before they woke you up and the therapy process to your eyes, and customisation to you seeing the right way. We were absolutely sure you were okay before you were dropped at the safe house for Barbara,' Belinda explained.

It took me some time to digest this all in. As much as it made sense, a lot of holes were still on the cheese that was my brain.

'Wasn't Dr V afraid that my uncle would get the hang of things after discovering that I wasn't dead?' I wanted to know.

Belinda shook her head. 'I'm sorry, Dean, but your father was the only male child in his family.'

'What?' It didn't make sense. *What was she trying to say?* I thought feverishly.

'What I'm saying is that you have no uncle that I know of,' Belinda informed me.

I looked at BJ and saw her expression agree with what Belinda had just said. *But how was that possible?* 'But, the Choirmaster, he told me that, he is –' I couldn't finish.

'The Choirmaster is in fact the person you call Dr V, Dean,' Belinda said.

The sudden information was just too much that I was afraid my brain was going to clot and kill me. *The Choirmaster is Dr V, but how? Was this another trick to get me to remember the eCodes?* I thought. My attention swerved to BJ. Her head was down.

'You knew about this?' I said, my throat sour.

'I got hold of Barbara a few weeks ago and explained what was happening to her. I helped her brother and family to escape from the other safe house yesterday and planned her escape today,' Belinda informed me. 'As long as you were at the safe house, the other men positioned as your bodyguards, or something like that, couldn't suspect anything amiss if BJ left the house. They would presume that she would return.'

'So you mean to say the safe house was just another bloody play?' I asked, trying to make sense.

'Yes,' Belinda said.

As she looked at me, I saw something in her eyes that made me very uneasy. There were no lies in them. Suddenly, I began to see things I hadn't before. Her features were sort of familiar.

'What made you believe her?' I looked at BJ. I was finding it difficult to accept the fact that phone calls alone would convince BJ. It was very queer to accept.

'I received a call from Switzerland from a man called Clive Montgomery. He is with Ozone Clouds. He convinced me to listen to your... er, mother,' Barbara said and shied away.

'How can you believe she is my mother?' I was quick to react. I didn't want this woman to be my mother. The only mother I ever had was Mr Parkinson.

BJ shrugged. 'If I didn't know, I'd have said you looked more like a brother and sister – there are some uncanny similarities here and there if you look closely,' she said. 'With the Choirmaster, you look nothing alike.'

If it was all true, it meant that the woman who had at one point shot me, this woman who looked exceedingly attractive and young, was my mother. It was all nothing, but incredibly insane.

'I know it's very difficult for you to understand this on one go,' Belinda said standing up. 'I will try to explain everything tomorrow after you have cooled down. I'll be in my room if you need me. Don't worry,' she said smiling at BJ, 'you are very safe here, nobody will find us.'

I was about to protest, but the stare she gave me shut me up. I watched her leave and the more I looked at her, the harder it was to give in to the idea of her being my biological mother. I was left with BJ who looked at me as if she was expecting me to burst curses at her any moment from then.

'Of all the people, of all the men out there, rich or famous, why me?' I said. I needed to know.

'Why rich or famous?' she answered with a question.

I shrugged irritated by the obvious response I was going to give. 'Don't tell me that every day of your normal grown life wasn't spent with more than a dozen men, rich and famous, reaching out for you, wanting you,' I said, not looking at her.

'And yet those days of my normal life passed and I've got only one man in mind, the man whose child I'm carrying,' she responded. 'Unfortunately, we don't choose whom we fall in love with. In the short time I knew you from working for your bank, going out – you being blind or not – I did end up falling in love with you enough to have you be the one who deflowered me.'

My prior theories of her working for Dr V and deceiving me had been much easier to understand. Now that they were now close to being asserted as hundred percent biased, I was confused as to why Barbara wanted me just as I didn't believe she did for real.

I had been a blind man to many when we had first met, she had known me blind, and yet she had gone as far as lose her virginity to me. She wasn't even shy to point it out. *Was she sticking to me for moral reasons, for her child to have a father present when born?* Now that I could see normally, was it a great coincidence to her?

'Why is it so hard to believe that I love you, Dean?' Barbara asked walking up to me.

I felt her hand on my waist, her budging belly pressed at my side. Deep down, I guess I was scared that it was true, that she did really love me. There were so many variables supporting her. I wondered why I was so terrified to be loved by such an amazing woman. She pulled me to the sofa and sat me down, then snuggled into me.

'I'm sorry, but it's hard for me to believe many things at the moment. Belinda, my mother, it doesn't make sense,' I said to her as I caressed her long hair.

'Why, because she looks so hot?' Barbara giggled.

I grinned. I knew that Belinda's attractiveness was possibly one of the things why I couldn't accept it. I figured my father to have been either a very handsome or a very lucky man to have been involved with Belinda, unless of course she had been a hooker as I had been told before. I was tired of thinking and let my mind drift slowly dozing away as I held my baby mama.

The questions, the answers – all had to wait. Enjoying the peace was good enough for me. Who knew how long it was going to last before something extraordinary happened again?

CHAPTER NINETEEN

The smell of coffee woke me up and, as I opened my eyes, I thought I saw Belinda looking down at me wearing a smile that was filled with uncertainty of whether it was supposed to be happy or sad. I closed my eyes for a few seconds and when I opened them again, she was gone.

'Morning.'

I looked up and saw BJ holding a cup of steaming coffee. She was sitting close to a window, apparently fresh for she had new clothes on. Her bulging belly made the buttons of the shirt she was wearing seem like they would pop off at any time.

'Hi,' I responded. I smiled for a while, and then the memories of my current position hit me hard. A sudden sadness fizzed through my body.

'Belinda said you sleep like a baby,' BJ said grinning.

I sat up at the sofa and rubbed my eyes. I wondered how Belinda felt every time she looked at me. So much time was lost. It was so heart-breaking.

'I'm really forgetting what a normal life, waking up in your own bed and making plans for the day feels like,' I said.

'I find that to be very ironic, Dean,' BJ said letting her gaze wander outside the window. 'I believe your life has never been normal from the day you were born.'

I wished I could see her eyes as she said it. 'I'm sorry you are in such a position,' I said regretfully. 'I know this wasn't what you had in mind when you thought about your future a year ago.'

BJ looked back at me and caressed her belly. 'Don't be sorry, Dean, life is weird sometimes, but I do know that there is a reason for everything that happens. I believe I am where I am supposed to be whether it is good or bad.'

I analysed her thoughts and thought a lot. *Was I where I was supposed to be?* I quizzed. *And for what reason was that if it was so?*

'What's next?' I asked absent-minded.

'We figure out our next move,' Belinda said suddenly coming into the room. She had a few papers and an external drive with her. She stationed herself at the room's desk and switched on her laptop.

'I hope it's not anything eccentric,' I said hopefully.

'Eccentric wouldn't be the word I'd use,' Belinda grinned. Many images lit up on the laptop and I found myself confused by each I saw. 'You'll need to have a stomach for this. BJ, please show the bachelor where the kitchen is. Preparing his own breakfast will surely freshen up his mind. I don't expect you to cook for him anyway.'

'Independent women, my ass,' I said rising up. Belinda looked at me and I looked away shyly, her attractiveness still getting the better of me.

'We're modern day Zimbabwean women, what did you expect?' BJ said leading me out from the room into the corridor.

We passed two doors on our way and she entered the third. The room was definitely not a kitchen, but had been coolly improvised into one. There was a small fridge, a smaller four-plate stove and a few cabinets and water containers.

'Here, find your way around. I've to visit the bathroom,' BJ said.

'Where is that by the way?' I asked. I knew that sooner I was going to need its services.

'You go to the west wing and it's in the second door from last. I'm sure you won't get lost,' she smiled and left me grinning back.

I searched and found the necessities and prepared myself a quick breakfast. It wasn't as good as those BJ had prepared for me at the safe house, but it was sufficient to help me acquire some much-needed energy. I chose to take my time before returning to the room where Belinda was. BJ popped her head in on her way back and left me with a smile on my face. I had feared she was going to want to keep me company, but I sensed that she wanted to spend as much time as she could with Belinda.

I figured it had a lot to do with her pregnancy. This was her first time and the presence of an older woman and mainly a woman for that fact was best for her. Since she couldn't see her own mother at the moment, Belinda was perhaps the best person to keep her company and calm.

My thoughts lingered on what our child was going to be like.

Was she going to be as stunning as her mother was? Was he going to be born with the genetic abnormalities I had had? I silently prayed, whether it was going to be a he or she that the child wasn't going to be what I had been. Whatever the case, I was sure BJ was going to love the child unconditionally. I wasn't so sure I would do the same, especially when I knew that I wasn't going to forgive myself for letting BJ have a child who was going to see with his or her eyelids closed.

I planned to wash my face before returning to the women. I climbed up the stairs of the west wing and ended up in an almost similar corridor. I must have forgotten the door to the bathroom for the one I opened led me into a nicely furnished room. I was about to close the door when something suddenly caught my attention. It looked like an album and when I walked in closer out of curiosity, I saw that it was an old journal. I opened it, and I saw photos marking a page.

They were photos of a young boy growing up. The photos showed the boy at different ages, the oldest being sixteen. The dark glasses on the boy made me assert with no doubt that the boy was me.

Most of the pictures included Ms Parkinson or one of my few prior school friends. The angle of the camera frames showed that they had been taken from long distances. Noting how incredible it was for Belinda to have restrained herself and watched her son from a distance as he grew, tears suddenly welled in my eyes.

'We wondered what had happened to you.'

I was so stunned that I dropped the journal. I looked up and as blurry as my eyes were, I made out Belinda standing at the doorway. She grimaced at my guilty expression.

'I'm sorry,' I stuttered, picking the journal and placing it where I had found it.

I helplessly tried to arrange it exactly as it had been. Belinda didn't say anything. She just looked at me. I got up and walked out of the room and this time did end up in the bathroom. I washed my face and stared at myself in the mirror. I looked weary and lost.

As I walked back to the other wing, I delayed my steps. My heart beat faster as I walked into the room where the women sat waiting.

'Dr V is an extremely intelligent person,' Belinda went straight to the point. 'For us to ever think of living normal lives, we have to take care of him first.'

'And how do you think we can do that?' I asked.

'Barbara and I have briefly agreed that the most efficient and quickest way to do so is to let White Haven take him in and that means you have to remember those eCodes,' Belinda explained.

'What have the eCodes got to do with White Haven taking him in or whatever you are suggesting?' I was curious.

'The servers hold quite a lot of information, a huge sum of it incriminating to those involved. Dr V and his associates know this and I think you have already seen the lengths they are willing to go to make sure whatever is in the servers is kept there. You have the key to that machine's doors and right now, only you can open it,' Belinda said. She looked deadly serious.

'I wish I knew how, I remembered how,' I said. It wasn't my fault that I had been memory-washed more than once.

'I don't mean to push you, but we are short of time,' Belinda pointed out. 'We can't stay hidden for long. Dr V has great resources dedicated to finding us at his disposal. We may only have a week or less to act and use the element of surprise.'

'I know that, but this isn't under my control,' I argued. I didn't like the pressure. 'I can't remember the eCodes.'

'But you remembered something?'

'Yes, but –'

'In all those instances, can you please tell me what caused you to remember? There must be a common factor and we can work on it to make you remember something,' Belinda was determined.

'I –' then I stopped. I remembered what had caused me to remember and I was embarrassed.

'What is it, Dean?' Belinda asked firmly.

I glared at BJ and shyly stared down. Belinda was curious at my reaction. She looked from me to BJ and then back at me.

'Oh,' she said.

'What?' BJ was left in the dark. 'Do you know?'

'I think I better leave you two together,' Belinda said and was out of the room before any of us was aware of it.

'What is it, Dean?' BJ asked concerned.

I couldn't tell her that a slight glimpse of her naked structure made me unable to control my nerves to the extent where a memory or two was triggered back. I stared down ashamed.

'Hey – look at me,' BJ walked toward me and raised my head by a finger on my chin. 'What is it?'

I was forced to look at her caring soft eyes and crumble. I told her and she blushed. It wasn't a comfortable moment for me either. I hid from it by going to sit at the sofa far from her.

Barbara stood there for a long time and then stared at the door. She walked slowly to it and closed it. She somehow guessed why Belinda had left us alone. She walked up in front of me and I looked up. She grinned and bulged her cheek with her tongue, her eyes creating a seducing light within them

I gulped endlessly as she slowly undressed herself to undergarments. I felt my body temperature rise. She walked to me and sat on my laps. As she started kissing me, I blacked out –

I woke up in my bedroom, at the house Ms Parkinson had inherited. I was looking out the window, my dark glasses reflecting the sunlight that shone through the window. I was gazing at the backyard and beyond. Ms Parkinson was cheerfully walking with our new neighbours, the Tariros. They weren't in a hurry and, from the way Mrs Tariro and Ms Parkinson were acting, it seemed like Mr Tariro was throwing jokes all round. It was a lovely sight, seeing the grownups laughing.

My gaze suddenly wavered and ultimately rested on something. From up there in the house, at first, it looked like a small statue, but as it moved, I suddenly made out a little girl. She looked tomboyish in her boy-like pants and t-shirt. It was the Tariros' youngest child, I realised. Ruth didn't look like the beautiful lady she was going to be then. She was full of energy and the way she lingered around the backyard made me sense that she was also very adventurous. I moved in for a closer look. My glasses must have created a sudden reflection at her for she looked up at my window. She stared for a while and waved. I waved back.

'Ruth, who is Ruth?'

I shook my head and suddenly regained my bearings. I was back to the real world. BJ was buttoning the upper buttons of her shirt and didn't look so pleased.

'What did you say?' I was confused.

'You mumbled *Ruth*, who is Ruth?' she asked.

I saw a familiar kind of jealous look from her eyes. I remembered her having that kind on a reaction every time we talked about other women. It was rather amusing that I couldn't help grinning.

I fought it down and put on a confused face instead. I told her about my flashbacks. She left the room in a dash and returned within minutes with Belinda on her heels.

'That was quick,' Belinda said surprised.

I chased the thought of my biological mother visualising me being intimate with a pregnant lover by immediately telling her that I had remembered something. We discussed if there was any significant link to the current setting. I think BJ was very determined to get the image of Ruth out of my head for she insisted on trying to make me remember again.

As I had feared, I developed a headache. I didn't hide it from them and Belinda suggested that it was best if I rested for a while. BJ grudgingly ended up agreeing.

'Don't worry, I won't dream of any small *Ruths*,' I teased her before dozing off.

The following days passed so slowly sometimes it was so frustrating. I tried all I could to hide my uneasiness, but BJ seemed to find it very difficult to control her moods.

Belinda told me that BJ was reacting to her current state and advised me to be patient with her. I avoided BJ as long as I could and forced my attention to focus on the little book. I wondered if someone like Mike would be helpful and suggested it to Belinda.

Belinda told me to that there was no way we could contact Mike without alerting Dr V's search for us. It was safer to leave Mike and his family alone now.

I knew that my remembering the eCodes was very essential and the most troubling thing was that what had caused me to have flashbacks no longer worked. I made out with BJ a couple of times, but it was no use. It appeared as if something had shortly inhibited my memory. Belinda was very patient, but I could sense that she was worried. Her White Haven contact was pressuring her to speed things up. The contact and his operatives were in the Zimbabwe, the more the probabilities of Dr V discovering him out and reading the situation.

CHAPTER TWENTY

The boy's mother stared down at her son for a while. It was five years now since the boy was diagnosed with the strange illness. It was a rare kind of genetic disorder. She had opted not to have any more children after Isaac, afraid she was going to produce someone like him.

The door to the room suddenly opened. Her husband walked in. 'How is he?' he asked.

The boy's mother smiled weakly. 'His condition isn't getting any better,' she said softly. 'Have you found it?'

The husband came over and comforted her in his arms. 'I'm trying all I can, Pam,' he replied with a shaky voice.

Pam snuggled in closer to him as she sadly stared down at Isaac. 'I wish I knew what it is you are doing, Andrew.'

Andrew knew that he could never tell his wife what he was doing, what he did and had done. All of it had led to this moment and now he didn't care what he was going to do as long as he saved his boy. A transplant was no longer an option anymore.

Years of extensive research had finally given him a breakthrough. He had found a way to cure Isaac. What now stood in front of him were only one man – and perhaps two women.

After all these years, he now understood why one of his most effective employees had gone rouge. By no doubt, Belinda would do anything to keep her son alive. He had feared that such a day would come when she started to respond to those natural feelings.

Isaac had little time left and what frustrated him the most was that he had found the solution to cure his son long ago, but couldn't access it.

CHAPTER TWENTY-ONE

I stood looking out of the improvised kitchen's window. Time was flying and no matter how hard I tried, I couldn't remember anything that I hadn't already. It ate me that every one of us was depending on my ability to remember the eCodes before proceeding to any vital actions.

Belinda was somewhere around the house whilst BJ was currently taking a nap. It was mid-afternoon and it looked lovely outside. Belinda had suggested that it was wise to keep indoors and avoid the risk of enjoying the outdoors to be possibly spotted by someone.

Staying indoors was tiring. I guessed it was also getting to BJ's consciousness. Belinda walked with her outside the house's backyard during the evenings so that she accessed some periodic fresh air and exercise. It was something, but I think it made BJ feel like an owl.

My attention was distracted by something black amongst the green. At first, I didn't take too much note of it, but its swift movement from point to point got the better of my curiosity. I leaned in closer to the window for a better view.

The sound of the explosion made me bang my head on the window and reel back confounded. Noises filled the house, the more amplified ones being shouts. I ran to the door and stopped when I heard gunshots. The gunshots seemed to originate from different dimensions. I waited at hypertension, away from the door. BJ's screams made me forget about all the dangers as I snatched the door open. Two bullets missed me, but the third nicked my arm. I took cover at one side of the corridor's wall and saw Belinda advancing towards two men wearing black. From the way they moved, I figured they were masked professionals.

Two other men were dragging BJ away. She was trying her best to free herself, but it was useless.

Belinda received a bullet on the shoulder and hit one wall. The gun fell from her grasp. I ran for her and without realising what I was doing, picked up the gun and fired.

The first shot echoed badly in my ears and the kick of the gun strained my wrist to almost numb of pain. I gritted hard as I fought down the pain. I fired two more shots and then stopped afraid that my untrained shooting would misfire and hit BJ instead.

The men fired at me, but as they retreated, I figured that they weren't shooting to kill me. Their shots were aimed at angles that were meant to scare me down. It seemed like they had got what they had come for. I took cover and pointed the gun at them, searching desperately for a clear shot. The fragments from the walls impaired my vision and the smell of concrete dust and gunpowder overtook me. I missed a step on the way down and fell after them. The mishap produced a stray shot that echoed away into the foyer of the house.

I landed at the base of the stairs with a grunt. The men stood there for a while as if making sure I was okay. One of them threw a cellphone at me and they left closing the main door behind. Seconds later, I heard the firing of a SUV's engine and its revving as it drove away.

I struggled to get up and pocketed the cellphone. I went upstairs to make sure Belinda was okay. I saw her carrying a suitcase and a bottle of bleach. She surprised me by cleaning drops of her blood with the bleach then winced as she threw a towel at me.

'Make sure you clean every part of the kitchen anyone of us might have touched. Hurry!' she shouted. She was holding her shot shoulder where blood stained her jacket.

'What about BJ?' I was hesitant.

'We have no time, Dean. Please do as I said, fast,' she ordered and carried the bag running downstairs. She picked up her gun along the way.

I did as commanded and before I knew it, we were in her car, a few minutes later. Belinda was hiding the pain, but I could see that even as she drove fast, she was feeling it. Considering the pain I felt from my own nicked arm, it was a wonder she was still alert.

'You need to see a doctor,' I said.

'We need to act fast —'

The cellphone I had in my pocket started ringing. It took me a few seconds to realise what it was. I answered it curiously.

'Hallo, Dean,' the Choirmaster's voice came from the other end.

I lost my voice. I had so much to say, but the amount made it impossible to get even one question out.

'I believe I have something that belongs to you, just as you have something that belonging to me,' the Choirmaster continued.

There was no hiding behind false masks anymore. It was now direct business.

'Why did you take her?' I screamed. Belinda glanced at me and slowed the car down. Her barely conscious eyes asked who it was.

'I thought you were going to say something like *"Why did you take them?"'* Choirmaster was as calm as usual. 'I have your girl and baby, you have my eCodes. You give me what's mine and I'll give you back what's yours.'

I didn't get a chance to respond. The van hit us hard on Belinda's side and as the car rolled over, I blacked out.

I could hear tiny beeps, but I knew I was dreaming. The dream was so vivid and for a moment, I thought I was awake. What gave the dream away was the fact that I was back at my house. I sat sadly in a corner watching as Ms Parkinson slept.

I didn't feel much of anything because I had known that such days was coming eventually. Ms Parkinson was an old woman. Unlike many, she had lived her life to the full. Not a day passed then when I didn't wish she had been younger when she had adopted me. The lady meant everything to me like nothing else. The future haunted me endlessly. *What was I going to do without her?* I would be left alone, all by myself to the wealth and attention of the sad world.

All of a sudden, I looked up from my thoughts and saw her sitting on the bed. She looked alive and energetic, her eyes gleaming with youth. I stood up and tiptoed to where she was, afraid that if I rushed it, she would disappear.

'Sit with me, dear,' she said.

My eyes filled with tears as I sat. It was a miracle.

'Don't cry, Dean, it's good to see that you can now see – normally,' she smiled. She looked so young when she did it.

'Is this real?' I asked although I knew the answer.

'What you want it to be is what it is, my child,' Ms Parkinson put her hand on my own.

'I'm dead, aren't I?'

'No, Dean, but it seems like you desperately want to be,' she responded.

I looked down. It was all true, I really wanted to die and leave all my problems behind. I wanted the peace Ms Parkinson now had.

'You have been strong all your life, Dean, why stop now? You were born special. I always knew that you'd grow up to be unique and it saddened me that I was never going to enjoy those moments, see you become the man you are now.'

I sniffled hard. 'And you must see what I am now. I can't take it anymore. It's just too much.'

'If you give up, what about Barbara, your child and Belinda? You are their hope and they believe in you.'

I shook my head sadly. 'How can I help them now? The only way I know how is beyond me. I simply can't remember the eCodes. I have tried, but I can't.'

Ms Parkinson smiled at me. 'You remember where the eCodes are, Dean, you have known all along.'

'No, I don't,' I was defensive and my tone stunned me. It was as if I didn't believe myself.

'Yes, you do. You're a gifted human being, son. You're also still human. Before you see it, I guess you have to ask yourself why you are afraid.'

'Afraid of what?' I didn't understand.

'Why you are afraid that by remembering who you used to be, afraid that by remembering the eCodes, the future will change dramatically. The eCodes aren't the way to solving your problems, Dean, you know it too. You no longer have an identity. You have a new life. Wouldn't you give anything to live that life?'

I woke up with a start and the pain hit me hard. The face was foreign to my memory, but its smile was warming. The pain didn't leave me though and the more I opened my eyes, the greater it was. I tried to get up.

'No, no, sir,' the nurse said. She pushed me down gently.

'Where am I?' I asked confused.

'The main hospital, sir. You were involved in an accident yesterday,' she said with trained ease and calm.

'Belinda, Belinda,' I panicked.

'Don't worry, sir, your wife is okay. She is recovering well,' the nurse assured me.

'My wife, oh,' then I remembered. Belinda had surely been

mistaken for my wife. It was a relief to hear that she was still alive.

'Your father has been worried sick. I'll go and tell him that you are awake,' the nurse smiled. She left before I could object and tell her I had no father.

When he walked in, I wasn't the least surprised. I suddenly believed that he was one of the not so many people who would lose a lot with me dead. If I died, the eCodes would die with me. The Choirmaster walked slowly to my bed.

'You?' I tried to act surprised.

'Of course me, Dean, what did you expect?' he said. He stopped a few meters from where I lay.

'Where is she? What did you do with her?' I heated up.

Choirmaster smiled ironically. 'Which she, your mother, or your girlfriend?'

I didn't say anything. The hatred within me consumed my vocal ability.

'Miss Maya, we already know that she is safe with me – for the time being,' Choirmaster said. 'As for Belinda, well, she is lying in the next room. Division is very eager to have her awake to ask her where she got that bullet wound and also the gun found in your car and cash. It's lucky you are John Doe now. When we killed your identity, we were smart about that. It has paid up today.'

So many questions were on the tip of my tongue. I didn't know which to ask first.

'Your mother was going to be a big problem. It's good she is out of the picture right now. We can carry on with what we started. The eCodes, Dean?'

'I don't remember any eCodes,' I said.

'You don't have to remember them – you possibly can't remember them all. You have to remember where you hid them.'

I looked at him confused. 'What are you talking about?'

Choirmaster smiled. 'The eCodes can only be stored on three data cards.'

Nobody had told me this before. *Was I expected to know?*

'My son doesn't have much time, Dean, so I'll give you up to ten in the morning tomorrow to deliver. If you don't, I'm afraid the price for my son leaving me will be your girlfriend and unborn child.'

Choirmaster left the room before his words were clear to me. I shivered badly and my injuries started to hurt. The nurse suddenly appeared wearing her ever-appealing smile. She injected something in my IV line for the pain. I recovered slightly.

I remembered dozing off to sleep and waking up later. It was now dark and I figured it was nighttime. The hospital's robe that I wore felt moist. There was a peaceful silence all round. The silence made me think a lot, most of my thoughts centred on my mother, and how I was going to do as the Choirmaster requested. It suddenly dawned on me that I knew where the eCodes were, I had known all along. The dream had opened my eyes and it was so amazing how easily I could remember.

I had had many hunches that the key to my memory was my old mother. Ms Parkinson had showed me the light even though she was gone now. Her spirit had guided me through to where I was alive and I couldn't be more grateful.

I looked around and made my decision. I had to see this through to the end. I carefully removed my IV line and searched the room for any clothes. I found a white uniform that must have belonged to a male nurse. It was old and the trousers barely fitted me. I searched for shoes, but found none.

After moments of hesitation, I peeped out of the door and saw that the corridor was partly empty except for a nurse and police officers. The two were chatting at the reception area a few meters away. I used that opportunity to sneak into the next room.

Her peaceful appearance caught me unawares. She looked exceptionally pretty with her long hair spread over her pillow. I grimaced as I walked over, sadness draining me. She had a bandage on her inner shoulder stained by a little blood. I guessed it to be the bullet wound.

I looked for and didn't find injuries that could have developed from the accident. Subconsciously, I found myself standing beside her bed and holding her weak hand.

I peeped out of the room minutes later and saw the police officers and nurse busy in conversation. I knew that they would be at it for a long time for they surely needed each other's company in a silent hospital.

With only a shirt and trousers on, and a pair of slippers I had somehow found at the hospital, I was struggling with the chilly night's weather. I walked around the Avenues like a strange homeless man. The effects of the accident began to wear me down.

As I walked along an area just adjacent to the fringes of the Avenues, I ended up where prostitutes were looking for clients. I knew that one of them was probably going to be my only chance for help.

Some of the women in tight hugging skirts glanced at me and were undecided on how to categorize me. I guess my looks and my dress code differed totally. I took my time to choose and later approached a young woman whom I was sure didn't look her real age and was on her own, having apparently appeared out of the dark.

'Hi, honey, are you looking for a quick screw?' she said smiling at me. She made sure she strut all of her assets for me to see.

I nearly chocked staring at her desperation to make a few dollars off a stranger.

'Don't you like what you see?' she was a bit offended by my negative response.

'No, it's not that. I'm looking for help,' I said, not taking my eyes off her.

'Help?' she was stunned.

I saw that she was slowly mistaking me for a vagrant. I made an effort to smile at her. 'Do you have a phone on you?'

She studied me for a while, undecided on her next reaction. I kept my smile as constantly even as possible. I breathed a sigh of relief when she produced an iPhone from her purse.

'Thank you very much. I won't be long,' I said and walked sideways. I called the Choirmaster.

'Dean, my boy, I didn't expect to hear from you so soon,' the Choirmaster said from the other end.

'If you want the eCodes, I want something else in return,' I said.

'Anything you want, Dean, name it.'

'I want you to leave me and my family alone. My wife, my mother, my child and I,' I was very direct.

I didn't know how much money the phone held in its account balance and how patient the young prostitute was. I glanced at her. She was eagle eyeing me from a distance with her arms crossed.

'Your wife, ahhhh. Okay, Dean, I give you my word,' the Choirmaster made sure I knew he was in control as his voice sounded as calm as mine was totally the opposite.

'First of all, I need transport. Send me a driver at,' I looked around and picked up the street I was in. I gave him the directions and hung up on him. He had no choice, but to follow my orders.

I shivered some more as I walked back to the young woman.

'Thank you very much,' I said handing her phone over, a weak smile on my face. It was very difficult to smile when my body was in pain.

'Hey – wait a minute!' the young woman said. 'I've seen your face before, it looks very familiar. Ah, yes, I get it. Are you related to that banker who was in the news a month ago?'

I was stunned and tried my best not to show it. I guessed that I didn't look like the publicised version of myself mainly because I no longer wore dark glasses.

'People say I do look like him, in a way,' I devised my story. 'I guess we are somehow related.'

The young woman looked very excited. 'What's your real name?' she asked.

'Zvikomborero Shava,' I said at whim. I looped the name in my head repeatedly. 'You?'

She looked hesitant and I figured she was quizzing on whether or not to lie to me. 'Fortunate Guzha,' she said frowning. I figured that was her real name.

'How old are you, Fortunate?' my curiosity got the better of me. It was a direct question and only was it aware to me when I had already asked it.

'Eighteen,' she frowned some more.

She felt like she couldn't lie to me. I looked remarkably innocent in her eyes. She was as young as I had estimated. Her body had matured fast and I was stunned by how beautiful she looked when you visually stripped her off the makeup and seducing clothes.

'What?' she asked with an uncomfortable look on her face.

'Why do you do this?' I asked.

'Don't you dare judge me? Look at you, vagrant,' she was defensive. Tears stained her eyes almost rapidly.

We both knew that I wasn't a vagrant although I almost looked like one. 'I am not judging you. I'm just asking.'

'As if you'd care. I have studied you men. You're filthy creatures, insatiable idiots.'

Her vocabulary surprised me. Her tone as she spoke was that of an educated individual. I noticed something about her posture. It was too solid for her profession and she never maintained eye contact for more than a few seconds.

'You can't be satisfied about what you currently have, but you can happily look forward to what you can have,' I said looking down. 'My life is a good testimony of that.'

Fortunate's gaze unsettled me a little, lingering at my feet. 'What's your story? Why are you in a nurse's uniform?'

I didn't know how to respond. I just looked at her. This time she didn't look away. She looked back at me waiting for an answer. Only then did it dawn on me.

'How long have you been a journalist, Fortunate?' I asked.

Even though she tried to hold her position, I knew. I had hit a bull's eye. Her disguise was almost perfect and anyone would have given in to it except those who had tried it before. Having known Ruth for many years, she once had an exclusive story by acting as a prostitute. Over the years, a few young women early into the industry of media had tried to imitate her and none had succeeded.

'Who are you really?' Fortunate was shocked beyond recovery.

'You are waiting to expose some big businessman or politician for hiring hookers, aren't you?' I asked on top of her question.

Fortunate squirmed. 'How do you know all this?'

'Real prostitutes don't have thousand dollar phones and work at places such as these. They don't use dictionary vocabulary, look twice at someone dressed as I am and, mostly, don't ask many questions,' I enlightened her.

'Are you a pimp?' she asked.

I grimaced. I knew it was a joke and enjoyed her humour whilst it lasted. 'Don't waste your life trying to be what you are not, Fortunate. Life is short,' I said.

Fortunate eyed me with eyes filled with curiosity. If her evening was dedicated in some plot to expose some conspiracy, I knew that it was now turned to satisfy her curiosity. 'Please do tell me who you are.'

'I told you who I am already,' I said and started to walk away.

She followed me and it became annoying, as she didn't leave me when I told her to.

A black SUV suddenly came from nowhere and parked in front of me. It was followed by another black sedan. The driver of the SUV got out. I remembered him as one of the gardeners at the safe house. He handed the car keys at me.

'Your transport, Mr Parkinson and the Choirmaster has made

sure you have everything you may need in the car,' he said and walked over to the sedan.

The sedan sped off with him. I stood there gazing at the SUV. The Choirmaster had delivered, now it was my turn. I knew that I had a lot of time before our meeting the following day.

'Jewel Dean Parkinson, I should be damned.'

Fortunate's voice shocked me awake. I turned to look at her and saw her face beaming with excitement. It was a story of a lifetime. It was like a miracle to her.

I walked over to the car and got into the driver's seat. Before I could start the engine, the passenger's door opened and Fortunate climbed in. She closed it and immediately buckled herself.

'What the hell? Fortunate, please get out!'

'Zvikomborero Shava my foot. You are the Blind Banker. I knew it. You aren't dead – I knew it,' she bubbled in the seat.

Her long slit skirt made me have a glimpse of some skin and oddly, it didn't have an impact on me as I thought it would. *Was I now immune to my sexuality?*

I knew there was no way I was going to get this determined young lady out of the car without physically handling her. I thought hard for a solution.

'If I am the banker, then you must know that I killed the Tariros, that I am dead.'

'If you were all those things, I'd have run the moment I knew. Killers who kill the way you are rumoured to have murdered Ruth's parents don't ask politely for cellphones from prostitutes and say things you said to me earlier. They definitely might look as handsome as you look, but they wouldn't wear a nurse's uniforms like a disorganized mental and call for undesired attention.'

I didn't know what was more offending, that my character couldn't convince anyone like this lady that I was a criminal even though I had made it to be the most wanted man in the country or because the Choirmaster had thought I needed more incentives by having a small framed picture on the dashboard.

'Who is she?' Fortunate took the picture.

'I don't think you know what you are getting yourself into, Fortunate,' I said.

'She is very beautiful. Is she Zimbabwean?' she ignored me.

I snatched the photo from her and threw it to the backseat. Fortunate glared at me.

'Are you out of your mind?' I said.

'I know what I am getting myself into, Jewel Dean. If it makes me the Queen of Zimbabwe's Media, I don't care if it kills me. I don't like being in Ruth Tariro's shadow all the time.'

'But you are only eighteen, why the sudden rush to be gold in the industry when there are like more than hundreds out there trying to be what you want to be and have more experience and exposure?' I was confused.

'To be the best, you have to want to be the best. Age and experience are just aspects of non-importance when it comes to making it in the practical world.'

I stared at her. *Did she know that Ruth had been my best friend?* I saw the ambition in her eyes. She was only a teenager and yet she saw herself competing with the best of the best. Her impatience to wear the crown clearly showed. That ambition must have clouded her perception because what I was involved in was beyond normal.

'This is Conspiracy 101, Dean, a story of great proportion. Exclusive rights to your story will make me unbeatable and who says by twenty-five I won't be the next Oprah?' Fortunate was unmoved in her goals.

I shook my head. My life couldn't get weirder. Here I was arguing with an eighteen-year-old of all things. 'You don't have the slightest idea what want to get yourself involved in, girl,' I was no longer negotiable. 'Trust me when I say, you don't want to.'

'What are the chances that on my search for a good story, Jewel Dean Parkinson, the famous blind banker, murderer and dead suddenly comes to me and asks for my help? What are the odds that of all the people you met today, you met me? I didn't become what I am today by letting such things pass me, I am resilient.'

'You are –'

'Oh no, you don't,' she cut me off. 'You even know *the Choirmaster* and that on itself points out to a huge conspiracy. I had no idea the name had a real person behind it. You asked for my help, Dean, and this is me helping you.'

It was an argument I knew I wasn't going to win. Ruth had the same character and it was a waste of time trying to reason with a journalist. Somehow, I knew that sometime later, I would need someone like Fortunate. However, taking her with me was very risky. There was no telling how far she was willing to go and the further she went, the less her life was safe. The second from last thing the Choirmaster wanted was the media. Fortunate had no connection to me and I knew the Choirmaster wouldn't hesitate to expire her the moment he knew about her.

'I can't guarantee your safety, Fortunate,' I told her.

'Dean,' she rolled her eyes and I involuntary smiled at the way she did it. 'They framed you as a psychopath murderer, they had a million-dollar payoff on your head, killed you and God knows what. I know that being with you right now is like signing a death sentence on myself.'

I hoped she really meant it. I couldn't have the lives of two women on my conscience. I knew that if anything irreversible happened to Fortunate, I would never forgive myself. It was worse with BJ, but BJ was already consistent in the picture.

I nervously drove from the city towards my former house. It had been years since I had driven a car – most of the driving, which I had done when I was alone at the house. For the first few minutes, Fortunate was very silent. I guessed that the reality of what was happening had caught up with her. Part of me wished she would ask to be dropped off after changing her mind. The rest of me wanted company and wishing that if I didn't make it, someone else would to tell my story to the world.

'Did you know Ruth?' she asked.

I nodded my eyes on the road.

'Ruth used to talk about you a lot, especially after you gave her an exclusive on the opening of Silver Bond Market Bank. I thought you gave her the story mainly because you lived in the same neighbourhood. But after her parents were killed and she didn't make it a secret that she believed you were innocent – even after her uncles put up that crazy reward money, I knew you must have been close.'

'We were. She was the only young child just as I was – in such a big, but deserted neighbourhood,' I simply said.

We could have been married if I hadn't met the Choirmaster. Whether my life retained its normality, I knew that chapter of my life was irreversible. BJ had appeared in my world and there was no way of getting rid of her.

'Were you ever blind?' she asked.

I knew it was a question she had been dying to ask for a long time. I told her some of my story and from the lack of interruptions, I knew that she was too shocked to say anything or too unresponsive to whether believe if my story was true or not.

CHAPTER TWENTY-TWO

The evening was chilly as it neared seven, mainly because of the windy conditions. It was a while since I had been at the house, but only a few things had changed. One of my secret walking paths to the house was covered with dry brown grass showing lack of its usage for quite some time. I remembered using the road a lot during my childhood and a few times as man. It led directly into the orchard from a small-undeveloped field, which had recently been purchased, by a church.

I parked the SUV at a secluded area where three trees were rooted. I tried my best to select a spot where the car wouldn't look suspiciously foreign to any passers. I looked at Fortunate and witnessed the anxiety she felt by her absent gaze.

'Are you okay?' I asked.

She looked at me and smiled nervously. She nodded, but I knew that she was now not as confident as she had been minutes ago. I knew that her turning back now would really eat up the few precious hours I had left. I regretted my weakness of not having been firm with her.

I searched for a flashlight in the SUV and found one. It was all I needed for my expedition. I suggested that Fortunate wait for me in the SUV and she agreed.

As I was about a few meters away from the car, on my way towards the direction where the secret path was, I heard soft footsteps running towards me. I looked back and swore.

'What are you doing?' I asked heatedly.

Fortunate reached me and grinned like a silly schoolgirl. 'I simply can't wait in that car. What if something happens to you and you need help?'

I screwed my expression, impatient. I got hold her arm and dragged her away with me. *What could possibly happen?* The house would surely be deserted. I knew that the Choirmaster had no reason to have his men around the house watching out for a possible sudden appearance from me now. If his men had been around, I was pretty confident they were no longer stationed there. With BJ in his custody, the Choirmaster knew very well that I would give him the eCodes without hesitation.

'Why didn't we just use the gate?' Fortunate was curious. I was sure she had my kind of assessment of the situation.

'It maybe evening time, but imagine if we are to come across anyone? Possibly neighbours?' I pointed out.

'Oh, you are dead. I had forgotten.'

I didn't want to meet anyone familiar. I knew that it would only complicate things. Prevention was after all better than cure.

'That's Ruth's house?' Fortunate asked. She was pointing at the Tariros' backyard. From where we currently were, we could see parts of the house.

I thought about Ruth. It was now more than two months since her parents died. I wondered how she was holding up. To Ruth, I was dead, there was no question about it. My feelings for her intensified with each thought, with each question.

How would she react when she discovered that I was alive and currently had her adversary with me? How would she react when she knew that I could see?

As I had expected, the house was locked. I searched for a spare key I had kept under a flowerbed. It looked as new as it had been when I had put it there years ago. I had never dreamt that the first time I would use it would be when I no longer owned the house. The key belonged to the backyard door. We carefully made our way to the backyard. Much to my relief, the locks hadn't been changed. Dust was all over the place, but every asset was still in it. We passed through the kitchen and climbed the stairs to the wing where my bedroom was situated.

'Lovely house,' Fortunate said with amazement.

I murmured *"thanks"*. It was sad enough to be at the place and worse because I had to endure the fact that everything in the house no longer belonged to me on an official basis.

We entered my bedroom and I didn't linger. I did exactly what I had planned to do in the car. I packed a suitcase with all of my most important possessions.

'How old are you?' Fortunate surprised me. I had almost forgotten she was around.

I stared at her and saw her scanning the room and its belongings with interested eyes.

'Why?' I asked.

'I don't know,' she said, picking up Ms Parkinson's photo from my dresser.

'Please give me that,' I said rather harshly.

Fortunate stared at me and handed the photo over. She held it for a few seconds before letting it go looking at me directly in the eyes.

'I have seen photos of only two women in this room and not even a single man. You haven't told me everything, have you?'

I continued packing, annoyed by the sudden interrogation. 'What is that supposed to mean?' I was defensive. Of course, I hadn't told her everything. I barely knew who she was, less of all trust her.

'You told me that the Choirmaster has got someone special to you under hostage.'

'I told you no such thing,' I shrugged.

Fortunate frowned back. 'You didn't say it out loud, but then I'm a journalist. You underestimate my intelligence, Dean. That photo left in the car and everything you told me. Come on, I'm not that stupid.'

'I never said you were,' I said, not daring to look at her.

'How come you don't have pictures of that lady, not even one framed in here like the others? I see that you got Ruth's picture in her graduation gown and that old lady's. The old lady, I can understand.'

'So what are you implying, Fortunate?' I didn't give in to her. I wanted to hear what she thought she knew first.

'I'm not implying anything, but I'd like you to tell me things. I don't like walking in the dark.'

'Okay, lady,' I zipped my suitcase. 'I'm sure you know what ransom is. That lady in the picture happens to be carrying my child. She is called Barbara. The Choirmaster is holding her and wants the eCodes in return. I happen to know Ruth almost all my life, she is or was my best friend.'

The last part seemed to rock her. She kept staring at me as if waiting for me to say something other than what I had just said. I had told her what I thought was what she needed to know not what she was supposed to hear.

'And you trust the Choirmaster is going to let her go, just like that?'

I had not thoroughly thought about it, but I was doubtful the Choirmaster was going to let BJ and me go after all we knew now.

'I don't think so,' I replied truthfully.

'So why give him the eCodes?' Fortunate said gesturing her hands in disapproval. 'You aren't planning to hand them over, are you?'

'What choice do I have?' I asked.

'What about this Belinda person you were talking about and the White Haven Agent?' Fortunate suggested.

I hadn't told her who Belinda really was, but she knew just enough. I thought of my biological mother lying hurt in the hospital. There was nothing she could do about this situation anymore. It was up to me. Fortunate sagged inwards on my lack of response.

I looked outside the window and thought of Clive Montgomery. I was confident he was currently looking for us. *How could I contact him without alerting the Choirmaster?* First thing first, I needed to get the eCodes.

'Can you stay here for a while,' I said, turning back at Fortunate. 'I need to do something fast.'

Fortunate opened her mouth to ask something, but closed it and nodded slowly. I left the room and then left the house in a hurry. For a second, I glanced behind me expecting to see Fortunate following me. She wasn't – for once, she had obeyed my wishes. With relief, I ran toward the cottage-like summerhouse. The area looked unbelievably neat. The summerhouse was built far across the yard, partly hidden by the orchard. It was like a small ranch-house in the woods.

Ms Parkinson and I used to spend our summers in it at a few days where the big house got boring, but we had mostly used it in winter. It was originally built in the early 90s using hardwood, but a few decades later, the summerhouse was burnt down by an accidental fire. One of the Parkinsons had later rebuilt it using real brick and hardwood coating the exterior and interior. It was a real beauty and warm habitat during the winter seasons.

I used another hidden spare key to unlock the summerhouse's door and I was met by strong humid air. It was clear that the room hadn't been used for quite some time. The place however looked like someone had been in it. I guessed it to be the police. They might have thought I would be hiding in it or hiding something useful back then.

For sure, I had been hiding something extremely useful, but nobody could ever know for I was the only person who knew this house inside out. I came out of the summerhouse thirty minutes later. I had what I had come for.

As I neared my room, I heard voices. I tiptoed cautiously and recognized that it was only one voice.

'What the hell?' I shouted as I entered the room.

Fortunate was stunned. She looked at me scared.

I went over and snatched the phone away from her. 'Who were you talking to?' I asked forcefully.

'I – er –' she stammered. 'My editor.'

'Are you insane?' I shouted at her. She squirmed under my tense gaze.

'I didn't say any –'

'What did you tell him?'

Fortunate nervously twisted her fingers together. 'I just, I just –' she stopped and tried to get her wits back. 'I just told him that I had a mind, a mind-blowing exclusive for him. I'm sorry.'

I read her and didn't know how to deal with her.

'You definitely know that any wind of this to the public and there is absolutely no guarantee we will succeed in this. You do know that?'

She nodded. 'I'm sorry, I was anxious of waiting.'

My temper subsided after a few minutes. I gave her her phone back and sat on the bed. She stood there, unsure on how to react next.

'The exchange takes place tomorrow at ten in the morning,' I said. 'I need to rest.'

I found solace on the couch. They were all dusty so I did a little house cleaning first on the one I was going to use. I suddenly realized that I hadn't taken any form of cover from the bedroom. It wasn't chilly, but I knew that during the night it would be. I needed something to cover myself up. I was truly surprised that I hadn't even changed into my own fitting clothes. The nurse's uniform felt tight, but it was now used to my body.

I collected all the sofa cover cloths and modified them into blankets. I removed the eCodes' datacards from my back pocket and studied them for a while. They looked exactly as the card Dr U had had. The card was now with Belinda. I wondered if it was a security access card as well. I hadn't asked Belinda about it. To think of it, I was still in the dark about many things. I hadn't asked Belinda a lot of things. Fortunate's phone started vibrating. I saw that she was receiving a call from some Hilt. I switched the phone off without hesitation.

The voice was sweet and consuming. I smiled.

'Dean, Dean.'

I woke up startled. Fortunate was looking down on me with an impatient expression. 'What?'

'It's eight o'clock.'

I rose weakly and felt my muscles ache like on fire. I lay back for a few seconds. The sun filtered into the room through the closed curtains. *Was it morning already?* I had slept like a baby and yet I still felt groggy.

'Did you hear what I said? It's eight o'clock?' Fortunate said.

She looked as if she had woken up on the wrong side of the bed with her hair disoriented. I recognized that she was no longer wearing a weave. Her hair was only twenty or so centimetres long. Her prostitute's makeup was no longer there and she really did look so attractive I was stunned for a while.

'Are you okay?' she asked.

'I am,' I said groaning, getting up with all my strength used.

'I'm sorry I overslept, it's almost time,' she said.

It suddenly hit me hard. I only had an hour to prepare to meet the Choirmaster.

'What now?'

I stared at Fortunate, confused. I didn't know what to do. I told her so.

'I've an idea,' Fortunate said.

'I'm all ears,' I said.

'Let's go to the hospital where Belinda is and I'll tell you the rest along the way,' she said.

I looked at her wondering what she had in mind, but couldn't make it out. 'There are police there,' I said.

'Don't worry about that. We need to go now,' Fortunate said and made her way upstairs. 'And please do change into some presentable clothes.'

Ten minutes later, we were dashing along the path from the house's backyard. I prayed that we would find the SUV intact. There was no telling what could have happened to it during the night. Luckily, the SUV was untouched where we had left it. Fortunate decided it was efficient if she drove whilst I carried out part of her plan. It was a sketchy plan, but it had potential.

'You love her, don't you?' she suddenly said.

'What?' I asked. I was staring at her phone wondering which call was vital first.

'You called me Barbara when I was waking you.'

I raised my eyebrows and bit my lip. Images of BJ filled my head. I forced them down in order to focus.

Fortunate took my silence as ordinary for she didn't say anything about BJ anymore. I could sense some faint strains of jealousy and was touched.

As planned, we passed by her apartment as she changed. In her normal form, she looked stunning. Although she was nothing compared to BJ when it came to appearance, I acknowledged her good features. She had chosen the right carrier path, I mused.

'Now to the hospital,' she said getting behind the driver's seat.

'Are you sure about this?' I said.

'This is the story of my life,' Fortunate said. 'I've never been so sure about anything in life.'

I hoped so because if anything was going to derail, I was sure that things would heat up. The level we were currently at was nothing compared to a situation whereby the Choirmaster discovered what we were planning to do before we actually did it.

CHAPTER TWENTY-THREE

Silver Bond Market Bank was where it had possibly begun. I was sure that it was where it was going to possibly end. The bank was rumoured to have been bought by a wealthy foreign business organization, but I knew that it now belonged to the Choirmaster. There was no way he was going to let someone acquire it whilst his precious research was still part of it.

The underground parking lot was purely lit at different dimensions. Fortunate and I had chosen the darkest of them all. The spot where we hid enabled us to observe who got in and out without being seen. It was beyond doubt that we were all very anxious. The spot we were at seemed to be radiating heat. It was a few minutes past ten and each minute brought with it waves of anxiety.

'I'm scared,' Fortunate whispered.

I looked at her and there was really no need for her to say it aloud. For someone who had thought of the plan, she surely didn't look so confident now. I put my hand on her shoulder. She jerked and moments later calmed a little.

Suddenly, indistinct sounds of cars arriving filled the air. We watched as a sedan and an SUV drive in and park close to the doors leading into the building. Four men, including the driver, came out of the sedan and looked around, surveying the place.

After a minute, one of them opened the passenger door of the SUV. Choirmaster came out, then BJ. Choirmaster helped her out and made sure she was okay. Choirmaster, BJ and the three men entered the building. The driver of the first car returned into his car and the two cars drove off. We waited for the discussed ten minutes.

'Are you ready?' I asked Fortunate.

She nodded. 'You didn't tell me she was pregnant,' she said.

I didn't remember if I had or hadn't told her about BJ's

condition. It didn't matter now anyway. 'Does it matter?' I voiced my thoughts.

'The plan had no pregnant woman in it,' she said stunned.

'Let's go!' I said and pulled her with me.

We cautiously made our way towards the basement door. I opened the door and peeked up the stairs. There was nobody around. I beckoned Fortunate to come with me, closely behind me. The meet was to take place in one of the bank's situation rooms. I produced Fortunate's cellphone and made the call.

The bank's interior looked old and haggard. I barely recognized anything about it. The thing that made me quiver was that it was deserted-silent. We knew where we were going, but the air felt stale and weary. I led the way to the situation room, trying to walk with more confidence.

It was difficult, especially when I saw two of the Choirmaster's men guarding the door to the designated room. I simply walked to it and opened the door. We walked into the room. Choirmaster smiled as he saw me enter. His smile however fainted when he saw Fortunate.

'Good to see you again, Dean,' he said. 'And who may you have here?'

I took my time studying the environment. At one corner, close to the window opened an inch or so, sat BJ. Close to her was one of the men standing diplomatically. Choirmaster stood at the middle of the room where there was a desk and three chairs. The room was dark compared to its usual standards.

'We are here and that's the only thing that matters,' I said trying to sound brave. I stared at BJ and looked away quickly. She had a worried expression, but looked unharmed. That was good for a while.

'The cards, Dean,' Choirmaster said.

'Let BJ go first.'

The Choirmaster snickered. He gestured to the man and he walked towards me. I walked back and he produced a pistol. It had a silencer screwed to its nozzle. I stopped. He holstered his weapon and moved toward me. He started to search me. He did so thoroughly, looked back at the Choirmaster and shook his head. The Choirmaster frowned and gestured his head toward Fortunate. The man walked toward her and she walked backwards.

'Don't you dare touch me!' Fortunate screamed.

Choirmaster stared at me. I looked at Fortunate and nervously nodded. We had no choice, but to oblige. The man searched her and the look on Fortunate's face showed that he was doing more than search. His expression didn't change, but he was truly enjoying himself.

The man looked back at the Choirmaster and shook his head again.

'I thought we had an agreement, Mr Parkinson,' Choirmaster said frustrated.

'We're going to do this on my terms,' I said.

There was a moment of tense silence. I knew that the Choirmaster couldn't do anything until he had the datacards in his possession. At the moment, I was the boss, but I knew that this form of restructuring was going to be taken as an insult later.

'Before we do anything, Barbara leaves with this lady,' I said confidently. 'They will leave this place unharmed, un-followed and only when I have full proof that they are far away safe, then we can talk business, uncle.'

There was more silence. I waited patiently. The Choirmaster later grinned. He knew I meant what I said. He nodded to his man. The man moved aside. BJ stared at him unsure.

'You can go, Miss Maya,' Choirmaster said.

Barbara tried to get up. Fortunate rushed to her assistance. They slowly walked back to where I was. I nodded at Fortunate and placed a caring hand on BJ. She tried to hug me, but with her now huge belly, it was apparently impossible. Fortunate walked out of the room with BJ. The door closed behind.

'Very good, son,' Choirmaster said. 'Very good.'

I stared reproachful at him. He walked away and went over to the window where BJ had been sitting, sat down and crossed his legs.

I stood where I was, thinking a lot. The first part of the plan had gone as desired. The next part was pending.

'You do have your father's genes after all, Dean,' Choirmaster said. He was looking out of the window as if watching something. 'I guess being born of Belinda as well, I can't say I hadn't expected you to get out of your shell and act accordingly. It's too sad we aren't on the same page.'

'And what page would that be?' I asked.

'The page where I have my goals and you have yours,' he responded.

'I thought my life was complicated enough when I woke up in my office with dead bodies of my best friend's parents lying on top of my desk. That was before I remembered everything you put me through, Andrew,' I said.

This got the Choirmaster's full attention. He stared at me shocked. I knew it was the mention of his name. I smiled inside. It was nice to see him disturbed.

'Why didn't you just carry out your part of the deal?' I asked.

Choirmaster shrugged. 'I was willing to give you normal sight, that was true, but then my old friend Lehnitz suddenly discovered what I was doing and everything changed. Lehnitz could tell you things about yourself that would have made you rebel against me.'

I guessed Lehnitz to be Dr U. 'Things like why Belinda worked for you and why she joined White Haven?'

Choirmaster returned his focus to outside the window. 'Something like that. Back in the days when Lehnitz and I were carrying out a special research on *Ultraviolet Spectrums*, we each specialized on certain projects. I dealt with the *Violet* part making me Dr V and Lehnitz on the *Ultra* part making him Dr U. Our researches were so farfetched we used quite a lot of money from OCC, funds which in the end we couldn't really account for without implicating ourselves. In our search for success, we had gone from lab rats to humans.'

I thought of what Dr U had told me and the book. It now made a lot of sense.

'Unfortunately, although the UV Project was meant to alter certain retina segments of human's eyes to give him remarkable abilities of extended vision, the people we experimented on had side effects serious enough to make them blind and eventually kill them within weeks. Through those years, we lost about a hundred and sixty-four people and when they finally discovered the truth, OCC thought we were imitating genocide. The discovery of this would surely bring the whole corporation down and they thought it best to extinguish us.' The Choirmaster breathed in heavily and held it for a few seconds before blowing out.

'Your father was a White Haven Agent at that time. In an effort to stay alive, Lehnitz and I managed to convert some of those Agents sent to expire our experiments and us to work for us. However, there was a big problem. Your father discovered that, in an effort to treat your mother for wounds resulted from a bad mission in Congo, Lehnitz had accidentally used your mother as part of the experiments. She was pregnant and of course, that only made your father's need for revenge greater. He was killed in the process just after you were born. Not knowing what you were born to become, we were forced to make Belinda work for us in return of letting you, a lab mistake, survive and away from OCC discovering about you. I was very surprised when she chose and gave you up to Ms Parkinson.'

I listened and my feet felt weak. The answers were finally here and they didn't taste so good. 'Why did you pretend to be my uncle?'

'Of course you know why, Dean, that's pretty straight forward isn't it?' Choirmaster looked at me. 'We had people watching you and we just thought you were born blind and owed your success to that white lady's wealth. As time passed, I carried out different experiments in search of a cure of a particular lung cancer. You must now know that I have a fifteen-year-old child who suffers from this ailment. I needed first rate resources to facilitate my research further and the heavens smiled at me when you wanted to start a bank. I had to get close to you, study you, use you and your bank and mostly gain your trust. Belinda didn't like it, but she had no choice, but to watch.'

'There are many banks out there, why mine?' I asked.

'OCC isn't stupid. It has its watchdogs consistently looking for us. I needed something off the radar, which couldn't get the attention of the government too. I needed a bank owned by a local, in a country whose system I was well familiar with. Over the years, I was careful to deceive the perception of OCC and got myself an influential reputation – what they call the Choirmaster, a solid ghost identity. With your bank, I recruited people like the Tariros to fund my research. Of course, I told them half the truth and they were ecstatic about a cure for lung cancer and the profits to come from it.'

'You used them, all of them,' I burst out.

'We all use each other in life, one way or the other. I am a Zimbabwean scientist, turned secret politician and puppeteer not by choice,' he said and shrugged. 'When I suddenly discovered that you could see with your eyelids closed, one day after our meets, it only made things more interesting. The lung cancer project needed more funds and I couldn't get them into your bank using proper channels, so at the same time I opted to have my research's servers at your bank, including a system that enabled us to pipe numerous illegitimate funds without anyone noticing at large. I used one of my men to contact you, promise you surgery to see normally.'

I was confused. All this seemed straight forward before it got complicated. 'Then why didn't you just go ahead as planned, why change it?'

Choirmaster remained quiet for a while. He knew that things would be different now if he hadn't changed his plan.

'I guess I panicked. Lehnitz got wind of my research and I knew that it was only a matter of time before he got to you. He somehow discovered that you could see abnormally and I think Belinda leaked that information to him. She didn't like how I was manipulating you. I knew that I had to take care of you before Lehnitz got to you. You were abducted the day after the party, forced to present the eCodes datacards. I was very convinced that they were legit not knowing that the other three you gave us were dupes. I ordered my men to programme you to believe that your mother was a prostitute and that your father had been weak enough to kill himself after your birth. We had to make you completely forget that you had ever worked for me and created the security to my system. You were difficult to break, but after two months, you finally crumbled.'

I fumed where I stood. Two months locked away like a lab rat was something that had me vowing this man dead. 'What changed?'

'You were very smart. I later discovered that the dupes were meant to penetrate into the system, multiply like a virus and develop a stronghold over the whole system as to later automatically shut the system down and request for the real codes, passwords or otherwise self-destruct. It happened directly after we finished the research and found a cure for my kid. It was a bad omen. All of a sudden, we couldn't access anything.'

I shook my head in disgust. 'So you tried to wake me up by making me a fugitive?'

'No, I didn't. I had to create a diversion whereby I'd become your saviour. The idea was to get you in trouble and rescue you. I was confident you'd somehow lead me to the eCodes. That I was certain.'

'Why kill the Tariros?' I asked.

'It was an unavoidable necessity, Dean,' Choirmaster responded confidently. 'The Tariros had warmed up to you during the years and they seemed to forget our main objective. They were used to stage your setup and erase any ties or investigations to my research, them funding the project and so on. Everyone was busy looking for Dean the killer not what his bank held. It was a *"two birds with one stone"* kind of a thing.'

I thought of Ruth's parents. It was a sad picture. They had been murdered for a cause they had believed in.

'There is something I don't understand. Why did you put all that reward out for me? Someone could have killed me and you'd surely have lost your research then,' I was curious about it.

'I'd like to take credit for that, but that was Dr U,' Choirmaster said. 'Things between me and Lehnitz didn't end up so well, you see. At first, we had the same ideas and ambitions. That was before his daughter was involved with one of our scientists. I was very reluctant about the relationship when he was against it. I assured him not to worry and keep his focus on our jobs and avoiding OCC from getting us. That was a very big mistake for the scientist was a silent sadist. He overdosed Lehnitz's daughter with some kind of drug during a sexual act. She died and Lehnitz never forgave me. We parted ways. When Lehnitz discovered about the research and my son having lung cancer, he wanted retribution. He knew what I had done to you, Belinda of course informing him. Therefore, he devised the Mr Tariro brothers' thing knowing that you were possibly going to end up dead in the chaos and I'd lose everything – at the same time betraying Belinda. Thanks to you, Ms and Mr Maya, you managed to survive.'

I moved a little. I thought of BJ and Fortunate. *Where were they now? Were they okay or had the Choirmaster's men ambushed them?* 'But Dr U got hold of me. Why didn't he just kill me then?'

Choirmaster stood up and walked a little towards the table. 'I guess he got smarter. He wanted the research for himself and turn you against me at the same time. The fire at the flat was supposed to kill Miss Maya to make the plan more efficient. If he later told you that I had ordered my men to burn the building knowing you weren't there, but Miss Maya was, you'd have undoubtedly snapped and given in to whatever he said. Wouldn't you have, Dean?'

I nodded subconsciously. I would have without an inch of hesitation. 'So it failed,' I muttered.

'Belinda somehow discovered about the plot and, you know

her, she couldn't take it. Unfortunately, she mistook you for one of Lehnitz's men during the fire as she searched for BJ not knowing that my men already had her safely away. Knowing what Lehnitz had done, she didn't hesitate to dangle you as bait, find him and shot him on the spot. Lucky for me, I had you back together with one of my eCodes' cards, the genuine one that was. We thought it was wise to give you your promised eyesight to facilitate your memory recovery – as per arrangement with Belinda. But then, Belinda had her plans further on.'

Finally hearing everything made me sick. It was too much to process, but it was better to know. My brain was now clear of clots of confusions. I could see clearly now – I could breathe without difficulty. It was a messed up situation, but I knew I would live through it. Out of all this, the only positive outcome was BJ and my eyesight. I had to fight for it and that meant phase two of Fortunate's plan wasn't going to go into motion.

'The eCodes now, son,' Choirmaster said.

'I told you, you'll get them when BJ is safe,' I said firmly.

'Have you ever played chess, Dean?' he said with a grin.

I didn't like the gleam in his eyes. 'What?'

'Always be five moves ahead of your opponent, son. That's a lesson we taught them that at White Haven. I'm good at chess, Dean.'

'What are you talking about?' I was near panic.

'Did you think I was going to let you get ahead of me, son? You really never had any control of this situation, Dean. If I had the power to have influence over a maid who has been with you for years, why do you think of me any less now? Fortunate has Miss Maya, meaning I have Miss Maya.'

I shuddered. *How could I have been so stupid?* It all suddenly played out for me in my mind like a whirlwind. Of course, like Mrs Maguma, Fortunate had been positioned to wait for me, systematically placed within my reach. She was one of Dr V's operatives. I suddenly remembered that she had been the one to come up with the plan, Dr V's plan. That person she had been talking to on the phone at Ms Parkinson's house, it was no Editor. It must have been Dr V. I now remember the signs. Her systematic placement near the hospital, her quick recognition of who I was, believing my story readily and offering me help. I had been played the perfect act.

'I now know where the eCodes are, son. Now I no longer have use for you,' Choirmaster nodded to his man.

'Please don't do this,' I begged. 'This will not do you any good – I beg of you, please.'

'I'm sorry, Dean, you have to die. Having you alive when you are officiated as dead does nothing to balance nature and possibly have OCC snooping around to discover me. Thank you for the services, my son will definitely live now.'

The man pointed his gun at me and ordered me out of the room. I obeyed and he told me to keep it simple as we walked down the stairs to where he was going to shoot me.

Chapter Twenty-Four

I did as requested by the man, following his directions, walking as judiciously slow as I could. I didn't want to give him any reason for using his gun early.

We reached the server room, which was guarded by two men I hadn't seen before. I figured that they had been there for quite a long time. One of the men opened the door for us.

The room appeared to be the tidiest of them all in the building, I noticed. Oval shaped, the server room had the mainframe computers in the middle surrounded by smaller workstations. The air was cool owing to the numerous air conditioners and powerful cooling fans that kept the system operating at a favourable temperature range. I was walked towards an isolated workstation. The station had six monitors fixed at various angels. It was the same workstation I had used to develop the Choirmaster's special system and the encryption codes' datacards.

My armed escort pulled a chair from one of the smaller workstations and gestured me to sit. I obliged. As I noticed and had expected, every computer monitor in the room had a red smiley face with black eyes and a black mouth. I grinned at the sight. I didn't remember if I had created that interface from scratch or had stumbled on it along the way.

The man stood aside and holstered his weapon. He put his arms at his back and stared ahead. He truly looked like a professional. I thought of the way Fortunate had played me and slumped weak in my seat. Before I could develop further thoughts, the door suddenly opened. Choirmaster walked in with a smug look.

'You really got a sense of humour, Dean,' he said. 'That, I will give you. I guess you inherited that from your father.'

It was no doubt an intentional mockery talking about my father. He must have known that I would be angered by this. As someone who had barely seen what my father looked like, it didn't reach the desired threshold of my emotions. However, I let him believe that I was offended by his statement by frowning.

'Call Wayne, Bill and find out if Fortunate gave him the accurate location of the datacards,' Choirmaster said to the man.

Bill nodded and left the room. I was left with the man who had made me believe he was my uncle. I wanted to spring at him and take my long stored overflowing revenge. I felt glued to the chair. There was nothing I could do without putting BJ in more danger.

'What will Fortunate do with Barbara?' I asked.

The Choirmaster grinned. 'Miss Maya will be held until she bears your child. Then after, we will let her go. Unfortunately, if your child is born with your traits, he or she will follow the same path as you. We can't afford to have any more lab mistakes, say another person who can see with his or her eyelids closed. That's if she or he is born like that.'

I fumed, suppressing my anger as hard as I could. 'Are you insane?' I burst. 'What gives you the right to determine the fate of a baby? What do you think you will prove trying to play God?'

'We have no guarantee what your child will be, son. If he is what you are, he will possibly be the seed to many future genetic anomalies,' he responded equally. 'Thus, we can't take that chance. I'm sorry, but sometimes we all have to suffer for the sins of our parents.'

Before I could argue, the door suddenly opened. Bill walked in.

'Wayne located the cards exactly where she and Mr Parkinson hid them before coming here. He said he will be here in ten minutes,' Bill said.

'What about the other issue, Agent Belinda?' Choirmaster asked.

'What?' I blurt out.

'Fortunate has left Miss Maya at the safe house under guard. She informed me that the White Haven associate has already been taken care of by our second unit,' Bill said and my heart sank. It had been Fortunate's plan and it was really working as she had planned. 'She is heading for the hospital as we speak to deal with Belinda.'

'What is she going to do to my mother?' I panicked. I didn't believe I was saying it, but I had actually acknowledged Belinda as my mother.

'A little accident with the hospital's equipment wouldn't be too much to do, son,' Choirmaster said. 'Belinda was dangerous enough with you around. After your death, I'm ashamed to claim that she will become a formidable force with nothing to lose. I've to commend her idea of contacting Montgomery. I didn't know about it, but then thanks to you, your trust in people has played a big role in my success.'

I had told Fortunate about Montgomery and Belinda. The element of surprise these two had devised for Dr V was no longer there. As informed, Agent Montgomery was probably dead and Belinda soon to be. Fortunate's plan, it was all about Fortunate's plan.

That morning, Fortunate had suggested that we visit Belinda at the hospital and try to get some information about contacting Montgomery. We had been lucky because Fortunate had managed to penetrate through the security of the police and speak to Belinda on my behalf. I had contacted Montgomery and we had coordinated on exposing Dr V first in the open during the exchange of the eCodes and BJ.

Montgomery and a few of his men were going to covertly survey the meet and when the time was right, arrest Dr V's men and Dr V at the same time. Fortunate had suggested that we hide the datacards at a particular location, enabling us to make the meet long and avoid ourselves from becoming expendable once the Choirmaster had the datacards. It was a very good plan.

'You have what you want,' I said bitterly. 'So why keep me in here, are you gloating?'

'No, Dean, unlike you I learn from my mistakes. You have fooled me once. I'm not going to let it happen again. I have to be perfectly positive that you gave me the correct eCodes. And if they aren't, I'm sorry, but the hands on the clock change position. I'll let you live and kill everyone you have ever cared for. Are we clear on that, son?'

I stared fiercely at him. I nodded slowly.

'Good,' he said arching his infamous hat's ream.

Silence followed for about five minutes. The door opened and in came a man wearing the same suit as the others. He had with him a small black case.

'Thank you, Wayne,' Choirmaster said receiving the case. He opened it as Wayne left the room. The cards were unmoved. I breathed in and held my breath for a while. Goosepimples irritated my flesh.

Choirmaster walked over to an isolated workstation and produced another card – the one Dr U had had and possibly Belinda had given him before my surgery. He inserted it into the first port. The system responded by a request for a passkey. Choirmaster typed it in. The smiley faded and an orange smiley appeared this time. Choirmaster took a card from the case and inserted it into another port after making sure it was the second one by small roman numerals inscriptions on one corner. The system prompted for a passkey.

'The key, son,' Choirmaster said.

The key was easy to remember. Ever since I had remembered where I had hidden the cards, everything else about them had returned like it had never been gone.

'*alpha66Victor8BravoAlpha917*,' I shouted out the key as he typed it in.

The system responded by the orange smiley fading away. A yellow one took its place. Choirmaster inserted the third data card into another port. A prompt for a key flashed on.

'*charlie40Beta6SusanPeter315*,' I shouted.

The key typed in, a green smiley appeared. The last card was inserted and I had to shout its passkey.

'*2peter74Bravo8DerreckLima212*,' I concluded with a tired sigh.

The system responded by rebooting. For a minute, I was scared that something had gone wrong. I watched as the Choirmaster stared anxiously at the monitors. Time beeped and he stared back at me, then back at the screens. Suddenly, the system responded with the rush of the fans whirling at tremendous speed.

It took three minutes for it to get into normal mode. The first thing the Choirmaster did was to check if his research and results were still intact. Ten minutes later, he sighed. Everything was just as it had been. He then checked the authenticity of the datacards. Minutes later, he was satisfied.

'Good work, Dean, good work,' he said.

'So what happens now?' I asked. 'You have got what you wanted. I'm no longer a threat or an asset to you.'

Choirmaster kept his attention focused at the system. 'That maybe true, but just to be on the safe side,' he said rapidly typing in various commands. 'I'll keep you unharmed for two more days as I let my scientists work on my son's cure.'

I knew that no matter what happened, he wasn't going to let me live after all this. 'Would your son approve of what you are doing to me?' I said in a sombre tone.

Choirmaster glared back at me. 'Leave my son out of this, Dean,' he warned.

'But you intend to kill my unborn child and me, all this is because of your son,' I taunted him. 'His survival will have blood on it. He will have innocent blood on his hands.'

I was struck hard on the face twice. I saw stars for a while from the blows. I was going to die anyway so I didn't care.

'What will his mother say when she finds out?'

Choirmaster furiously punched me three times and the fourth blow bowled me over to the floor together with the chair. I moaned and spit out blood from my mouth.

'Get him out of here and prepare him. We don't need him anymore,' he ordered Bill.

Bill helped me up and sort of dragged me out of the room. I was groggy, but I somehow made out where we were heading. It was towards the basement. Bill opened a door and pushed me in. The floor met me on the fall and it was icy. I barely got a chance to look around as Bill pulled me up to my feet and pushed me to a corner. I clattered into a pile of boxes. Bill moved to one corner and produced a long layer of plastic sheet. He made sure that it was positioned at the centre of the room – and produced his weapon. He checked the clip then the silencer. Satisfied, he gazed at me and motioned that I go on the sheet. I obeyed slowly.

'It seems like we have no further use of you anymore, Mr Parkinson. Please kneel facing the wall,' Bill said.

I didn't know what to do except pray and have faith in God's work. I was going to die after all. *Was I going to die a good man?* I was a victim of corruption, perhaps I would die a good man.

Not an innocent man, but dying a good man was good enough for me. If my actions and burden weren't going to affect other people like Ruth, Barbara and her unborn child, I believed that I could have died a better man.

I sensed Bill pointing his gun at my head. Then there was an explosion. Fragments of the door blew in and two silenced gunshots followed. Bill's body dropped where I had fallen. He was dead.

In the smoke and sparks of fire, I squirmed to see two men. They trained their firearms at me and seconds later withdrew their aim.

'Clear!' one of them shouted.

'Clear!' the other said.

His neck suddenly exploded and he crushed into the arm where the door had been. Silenced gunshots filled the air. The first man took cover, rushing into the room. I looked beside me and saw Bill's gun. From instinct, I took it and tried to get up. My shoulder was on fire. One of the fragmented pieces of the door had lodged itself into it. I bit my shirt as I pulled it out and later decided against it. It was keeping the blood in at bay. The pain was overwhelming, my eyes filled with tears.

The man scurried to one corner and gestured me to do so in another. His eyes were fixed at the door, his gun trained there. I scurried into another corner and waited, glancing to and from the door's way to the man. The air was filled with the air of echoes from the explosion.

Suddenly, one of the Choirmaster's men appeared and the man shot him twice. He dropped dead. Gunshots came from the outside. I heard people shouting *"clear"* from the outside.

'O3!' someone shouted. 'This is O2, are you secure?'

The man with me rose a little from his shooting posture. 'O2, this is O3, what's your status?' he shouted back.

'I have O5 and O6 with me, O1 is down!' O2 shouted.

'O4 is down too, but I have M1. Clear,' O3 said and he lowered his weapon slowly.

Three other men suddenly appeared. They were armed with the same guns as O3. One of the men rushed to me and saw that I was bleeding. He produced a bandage from my shirt's arm and began dressing the wound around the fragment.

'Mr Parkinson, we are undercover White Haven Operatives under the orders of Leading Agent Montgomery. Where is Dr Andrew Banga?' O3 said.

I was a bit taken aback. The pain in my arm didn't help either. 'He is in the server room. Three guard him.'

'Keep close to us, Mr Parkinson. Do you know how to use that?' O3 asked, pointing at the gun I was holding.

I had never used one, but I felt safe having one. I nodded. O3 was hesitant to accept my lie, but let it go.

O6 led the way to the server room. It appeared as if the team had schematics of the building for they cautiously scouted along the corridors with a clear destination in mind. I followed closely with O3 covering the rear. As we neared the server room, my heart beat furiously. I thought I was going to suffocate.

I barely realized what happened next except a bullet whizzing past me and hitting O3. Gunshots filled the air and the walls were assaulted, the air filled with concrete dust. The compactness of the corridors made the gunshots louder and deafening. We were under attack. I desperately looked around for cover and the next thing I remembered was ambling in a certain direction.

I opened the door and was met by a gunshot. The bullet caught me nice and neat right near the middle of my left hand's palm as I tried to duck for cover. I felt the searing of my flesh and the pain that came after was totally numbing. I pointed my gun and shoot. The *phhht* that came from the gun didn't satisfy my ego in the environment where gunshots filled the air. I kept on shooting until my clip was empty. Before I could process what had happened, I received a shot on the thigh. I fell down screaming. Then I heard clicks, desperate clicks.

An unbelievable calm came afterwards. There were no more gunshots, just echoes. I had a glimpse of the open door and saw dust filling the corridor. I knew that no one out there was still alive. I looked up with some effort and saw Dr Andrew Banga – the Choirmaster – frustratingly checking his gun to see it empty of bullets. He threw it aside. I looked around and saw that I had killed one of his men with Bill's gun and in the same process had shot three monitors of the isolated workstations. However, the workstation had survived my attacks.

'You see the problems you still cause me, Dean?' Andrew shouted menacingly looking down at me like a cat prowling a stubborn mouse. 'You have killed almost all of my security personnel and for what, Dean? Can't you just give up?' He kicked me in the stomach.

I groaned in more pain and wriggled on the floor.

The room was suddenly filled with caution sirens from the system's speakers. Andrew turned around and hurried to it. The surviving screams suddenly filled with some kind of code and the whole system started to corrupt.

'Oh, no!' Andrew said in a worried tone. 'No, no, no. This can't be happening,' he said, desperately operating the keyboard like a madman.

The system didn't stop. Instead, it increased in destructing itself like an uncontrollable virus.

Andrew ran to me and started to pull me up. 'Stop it, damn it, stop it!' he shouted pulling me harder.

I was woozy and didn't fight him. 'It can't be stopped. You lost that option when you used those cards,' I mumbled.

Andrew dropped me and dashed back to the system. He wildly operated the keyboard again, but it was useless. Everything in the system was being destroyed, every spec of data erased beyond recovery or recreation. Five minutes ended with the system ultimately crashing down and asking for an operating system to boot from. It was all over. Seconds later, the ports where the eCodes data cards were inserted self-destructed as the circuits overloaded and burnt.

Andrew stood there shocked and later fell onto the floor.

'What have you done, Parkinson, what have you done?' He had his head in his hands. I distinguished tears of grief. 'You have killed my son.'

I crawled to a nearby wall and leaned on it. I tried to stop the flow of blood from both my hand and thigh. 'You killed your son, not me,' I responded.

'You tricked me once again,' he said defeated.

'I did beg you to change your mind minutes ago and we all could have gotten what we wanted in the end, but you gave me no mercy,' I said wiping some blood off my mouth. 'I followed your advice. I was five steps ahead of you, just like chess.'

Andrew stared at me, his eyes red. 'What are you talking about?' he muttered.

'I learned a lot from you over the years, sir and the most important lesson of all was *never to underestimate or trust anyone no matter who they are.*'

The Choirmaster just stared at me confused.

'When I programmed those cards, I made sure that you were going to be true to your word and give me my surgery. I was dedicated to making your research legitimate and that was before you kidnapped me and forced me to work on the system faster. I created two sets of datacards, the ones that were to penetrate your system to later shut it down and the ones that would totally annihilate it. I planned ahead and hid the lethal ones just I case. They you made me forget and made me remember again. But from the minute I remembered everything I could, I was always ahead by three moves,' I said.

My revelations seemed to paralyze any movement of the Choirmaster. He stared at me wondering if I was bluffing or not.

'Your mother, mistress and child will be dead, that makes us even, but then my child was already dying. I was only trying to save him, but you lose everything from your life to what you had now. In the end, I win and you lose as always,' he boasted.

I shook my head and let him ponder with curiosity for a minute before I continued. 'No, sir, this is me beating you at your own game,' I said.

'I don't understand.'

'How could you? You are an ignorant son of a bitch. You could have avoided all this if you had played fair, but instead you tried to be selfish and gain all. I did get suspicious about Fortunate, so I called Ruth. She told me there was nobody called Fortunate Guzha competing with her or in her industry.'

'But Ms Tariro knows you are dead. That's a lie, Dean,' Andrew had a smug look on his face.

'Then again you underestimate me,' I said shaking my head again. 'One of the first things I did when Belinda told me the truth about you was calling Ruth and told her everything that was necessary for her to know without putting her in danger. Ruth and I have known each other for so long, she believed me. When I knew that Fortunate was fake, I told her everything, but then she already knew it all, so I played her.'

'Very smart, son, very smart,' Andrew said with a hint of being impressed. 'If you knew, why did you tell her about White Haven and let her take BJ?'

I was now feeling cold and possibly knew that I would die soon from the bleeding. I knew I had to keep myself awake in hope that some of Montgomery's men were coming as backup or something.

'I knew the only way to get her trust was to let her believe I believed her. When she came up with her plan of going to see Belinda and all that stuff, I knew what she was thinking on the other side. I knew that she wouldn't risk seeing Belinda if she was one of your people, instead she would fake seeing Belinda, tell me she had acquired Montgomery's number, which of course she would have received from you. I knew it would be easy since you are a very resourceful man and I wasn't wrong. I called Montgomery and informed him about Fortunate's plan, but at the same time I sent a text to him with a phone I stole from some kid when Fortunate was pretending to be visiting Belinda at the hospital.'

'Why did you let her leave with Miss Maya?' Andrew wanted to know. He was now looking very uneasy.

'First, to make her believe that she was playing me. On the other hand, I knew it was going to get hot here, so I wanted BJ somewhere safe. I managed to speak to Montgomery for a few seconds and he was to take Fortunate into custody after she told you where I had hidden the datacards. It's just as simple as that,' I said.

Andrew rose from the chair and pulled out some electric wire from the dead system. He pulled me aside and wrapped the wire around my throat. He started pulling hard as I chocked. My vision got blurry as I suffocated. *At least I wasn't going to bleed to death,* were my last thoughts. I thought I heard an exploding sound before everything in my world turned black.

Chapter Twenty-Five

The seasonal variations were hard to get used to, but then it wasn't that bad. Choices were made and some of them were not imperative or negotiable. It was a flow of the river, the current not subjected to plans, rules or limits.

I counted the trees and wondered if it was a coincidence. They were five trees and it was the same number of months that had passed since Harriet's second birthday. She had her mother's features as well as sweetness. I was proud of her. I looked down into the garden from the balcony and saw little Harriet playing with her cousin. Close by were Mike's wife and my own pregnant wife. I stared at BJ for a long time, remembering our history. I later looked away.

We were foreigners in this country and thanks to OCC – with their gratitude of solving their Dr U and Dr V problem – were living comfortable lives. I thought of my home country and knew that it would probably be years until we returned.

Mike had managed to convince his mother to come and live with him for a while. Mrs Maya had left Zimbabwe confused and every time I saw my mother-in-law, she had a question or two to ask about if I wanted my children to grow in another culture. She was planning on returning home after seeing BJ's second child.

I couldn't tell her that I couldn't return to Zimbabwe because of my tainted past, a past she didn't know. I evaded her worries by letting her spend lots of time with her grandchild at Mike's house. Somehow, she had made it her sole purpose to teach her grandchildren their culture and I had to admit she was doing a good job of it. Harriet and her cousin were now fluent in the little Shona language they knew. There was a sudden knock on the slide door behind me. I looked back.

'Hi.'

We exchanged hugs and pleasantries.

'How are you, Belinda?' I said, my attention returning to the people below us.

'I'm fine,' Belinda said following my gaze. 'She is growing up, isn't she?'

'Too fast, too fast,' I responded.

I glanced at her and slumped a little. Belinda's appearance still unnerved me. She looked more attractive as she aged. It had been very difficult to convince Mike and his family that she was my mother. Mrs Maya had thought she was my sister and to date mistook her as such if we didn't remind her.

'How is life at work?'

Belinda grinned. She owned a café in the quite areas of the country where she had met a charming local who was a pastor. When they had first met a year ago, I had thought it was a joke. Months later, they were married. I now had a pastor for a stepfather. It was a true revelation to me. I didn't expect her to respond and she didn't.

We let our eyes wander. BJ felt our gazes and looked up. She waved happily at us and we waved back.

'I never dreamed of such a day,' Belinda said smiling.

I looked at her and saw her hide her emotions behind tears. I knew she was happy. *Was I happy too?*

That question had vague answers. I didn't know true definitions of happiness. *Was it the calm after the storm?* I stared down at BJ and Harriet. I believed that whatever life had to offer for all of us, we were never really sure of the meanings behind the seconds, the minutes, the hours or days. What was really important was that I could see, my child didn't have any genetic defects carried from me and I had my mother standing beside me. If this wasn't happiness, then what you found in the oceans definitely wasn't water.

www.ingramcontent.com/pod-product-compliance
Lightning Source LLC
Chambersburg PA
CBHW051835170626
46807CB00003B/1193